M A

Ma's

BOY

MAMA'S BOY

Book*hug
Toronto, 2018
Literature in Translation Series

FIRST ENGLISH EDITION

Published originally under the title *La bête à sa mère* © 2015, Les Éditions
Internationales Alain Stanké, Montreal, Canada
English translation copyright © 2018 by J.C. Sutcliffe

The production of this book was made possible through the generous assistance of the Canada
Council for the Arts and the Ontario Arts Council. Book*hug also acknowledges the support
of the Government of Canada through the Canada Book Fund and the Government of Ontario
through the Ontario Book Publishing Tax Credit and the Ontario Book Fund.

 **Canada Council
for the Arts** **Conseil des Arts
du Canada** Funded by the
Government
of Canada Financé par le
gouvernement
du Canada | **Canadä**

 **ONTARIO ARTS COUNCIL
CONSEIL DES ARTS DE L'ONTARIO**
an Ontario government agency
un organisme du gouvernement de l'Ontario

We acknowledge the financial support of the Government of Canada through the National
Translation Program for Book Publishing, an initiative of the *Roadmap for Canada's Official
Languages 2013-2018: Education, Immigration, Communities,* for our translation activites.

Book*hug acknowledges the land on which it operates. For thousands of years it has been
the traditional land of the Huron-Wendat, the Seneca, and most recently, the Mississaugas
of the Credit River. Today, this meeting place is still the home to many Indigenous people
from across Turtle Island, and we are grateful to have the opportunity to work on this land.

Library and Archives Canada Cataloguing in Publication

Goudreault, David, 1980- [Bête à sa mère. English] Mama's boy / David Goudreault ;
translated by J.C. Sutcliffe. — First English edition.

(Literature in translation series) Translation of: La bête à sa mère
Issued in print and electronic formats.
ISBN 978-1-77166-382-3 (softcover)
ISBN 978-1-77166-383-0 (HTML)
ISBN 978-1-77166-384-7 (PDF)
ISBN 978-1-77166-385-4 (Kindle)

I. Sutcliffe, J. C., [date]–, translator II. Title. III. Title: Bête à sa mère. English. III.
Series: Literature in translation series

PS8613.O825B4713 2018   C843'.6   C2018-900816-4
                                                C2018-900817-2

PRINTED IN CANADA

"Even a stopped clock is right twice a day."
Conventional wisdom

In memory of Lucie Picard,
with a thousand regrets.

PROLOGUE

You've found the body. You have all the circumstantial and forensic evidence you need at your disposal. The case is closed, you've already drawn your conclusions.

But you can't come to a conclusion before knowing the whole story.

Here's my version. I'm being completely honest here. Maybe it won't change a thing. Or maybe it will change things completely. If it doesn't exactly excuse my actions it might explain them. Everything you need to know is in this file. This is where you'll discover all the extenuating and aggravating circumstances. I'll take my chances.

You'll think I'm romanticizing or playing the hero. In my memory, in my mind, this is what happened. It's my truth and that's the only one that counts… I'll let you be the judge.

I'll judge you too, in due course.

I ask that this document be filed as evidence and submitted to the jurors. I'm prepared to swear under oath to every paragraph.

1

RESILIENCE

My mother was always committing suicide. She started out young, in a purely amateur capacity. But it wasn't long before Mama figured out how to make the psychiatrists take notice, and to get the respect only the most serious cases warranted. Electroshocks, massive doses of antidepressants, antipsychotics, anxiolytics, and other mood stabilizers marked the seasons as she struggled through them. While I collected hockey cards, she collected diagnoses. Thanks to the huge efforts she put into her crises, my mother contributed greatly to the advancement of psychiatry. If it weren't for the little matter of patient confidentiality, I'm sure several hospitals would be named after her.

My mother was discreet, and usually tried to kill herself in secret. Contrary to what the official reports claimed, I wasn't all that bothered by her habit. Whenever Mama could drag herself out of her private hell and get back on her feet, she was a wonderful woman. And those experts can go hang themselves too, with their pseudo-analyses of our attachment issues.

The first time I found her, she was naked and moaning on the bathroom floor. I was four years old. Mama had hauled herself out of the bathtub, which was full of a reddish soup that made it look as though she'd been butchered. Her wrists especially. It was her sharp little cries mixed with sobs that woke me up. As soon as I dared poke my head round the door, she ordered me to go and get Denise. I froze. I'm pretty sure that's normal. My mother's nakedness, the steak knife, the bloody bath—it was quite the scene. But not really a satisfactory family situation, as people pointed out to me later. It was messy. I wanted to at least pick up the knife and put it away. My mother was awkwardly trying to cover her genitals and yelling ever more loudly. *Go tell Denise to call an ambulance, you goddamn imbecile!* Whenever the name-calling started, the slap was never far behind. *Go on, do it!*

Denise lived on the floor below. The triplex was poorly soundproofed, I always knew when she got up. She was deaf and watched television with the sound at maximum volume. I often ate with her. She kept a box of Cap'n Crunch specially for me in one of her kitchen cupboards. I used to snuggle up with Denise on her big brown leatherette couch. I'd try to follow as she compulsively changed the channel. When she hit the weather channel, she'd pause for a few seconds longer than normal. I found that fascinating, because she never went out—she even had her groceries delivered, including my precious cereal. But she still always knew what the weather was doing. *You never know, kiddo. You never know.* Denise was a wise woman.

What are you waiting for? You think I can go myself? Wake up! Mama had managed to get up and was hiding her bottom half by curling up between the bath and the toilet. I remember thinking she was going to a lot of trouble to hide a bit of hair. I hadn't really wrapped my head around the situation at that point. I was torn between throwing myself into my mother's arms, helping her clean up the mess, and doing what she asked by going to get Denise to help. *Go on, you fucker!* I ran to the neighbour's.

Every time I went over to her place, Denise would ask me to

massage her feet. They were all dry with white bumps and scars, but I indulged her. It was the sacrifice I made in our symbiotic relationship. Sometimes I tickled her and we both laughed. Despite the fifty-four-year age gap, I'd never had a better friend. She's the only woman who's ever told me I'm good-looking. I am good-looking, I know I am, but women hardly ever say it because I intimidate them. Denise knew how to win me over. She loved me, but there weren't many like her.

I hadn't put my boots on in the rush, and the iron stairs hurt my feet. It was a really cold November. Denise's door was never locked. I didn't even think about knocking as I burst into the house, calling her name. Getting no response, I raced straight to her bedroom and pushed at the half-open door. And then I was paralyzed with horror. The traumas were piling up.

Sitting on the corner of the bed, in the moonlight filtering through the blinds, her stupefied gaze meeting my own, Denise was holding her hair in her hands. Some distance away from her head. All that remained were a few tufts of sparse hairs. Her whole mane had come off. Gripping her scalp with her fingers, she stared at me, mumbling, *My hair.* She wanted to put it back on her head but it was already too late. The image had burned itself into my brain. Even more than the image of my mother's body on the bathroom floor.

Denise called the emergency services. I didn't dare look at her again. I stuffed my face with Cap'n Crunch until I felt like throwing up, waiting for my mother to go off in the ambulance and for someone to take me to a shelter for the night. I was grateful for that, terrified at the thought of staying the night at Denise's. If this bald woman really was Denise. I couldn't be sure of anything anymore.

After that, I often saw my mother try to kill herself, usually coinciding with changes in medication or partner, but I never saw Denise again. I have good memories of her, a feeling of safety mingled with fear. Ever since then, Cap'n Crunch has tasted of nostalgia, and I've had a phobia of wigs.

I know Quebec pretty well. I've moved way more than my fair share. All my childhood memories are linked to names of towns, which are in turn connected with the dramas that punctuated my youth. Shawinigan means Mama being poisoned by a medication overdose and the sounds of regurgitation. Trois-Rivières-Ouest was the tattooed René beating my mother up in the hallway of our apartment building. Sainte-Foy, the Xanax overdose and the ambulance ride. Donnacona, Mario hitting Mama in the middle of the street, and finally Quebec, site of the notorious hanging, where the shower-curtain rod gave way with an enormous crash as my mother yelled and swore.

The emergency services didn't come out every time she killed herself. This particular time it was the landlord, who lived underneath us, that showed up in a towering rage. He already thought, wrongly, that we were noisy parasites, but the din the metal rail and the body made as they fell into the bath had frightened him. He ran upstairs without even knocking to discover my mother battling with the dressing-gown belt around her neck and the curtain rod across her legs. Just as I'd done several years earlier in another bathroom, he froze. Which just goes to show that age doesn't matter; that kind of scene makes an impression.

I assume she carried on trying, but that was the last time I witnessed her attempting to end her days. We were definitively separated. For my safety and her mental health. To me, that seemed about as logical as trying to ban snow in winter or slush in spring. I knew full well she'd never die, and her lullabies were the only thing that could soothe me. We might have been an unusual family, but we were a family all the same. We needed one another. We didn't make it out of there fast enough. *Social services got us*, as she put it. I would have given anything to find my mother again, but seven-year-old children don't sit on multi-agency boards at child protection services.

They refused to tell me where they'd locked her up. I managed to steal my file once, but they took it back before I could get a proper look. A social worker let something slip one night when I woke up the entire building in the grip of my thousandth crisis. *Your mother was hiding out in the Eastern Townships. There wasn't any point though. She had another child, but we took it away at birth. You'll never see her again. Go to sleep!*

She must have committed suicide properly after that. She really loved children.

My father was probably an explorer, devoting his life to humanitarian aid. Or a welfare bum. He was also a drug dealer and a karate teacher. He could have been anything, actually, since I never even knew who he was, never mind what he did. My mother told me he was either called Marco or Louis. In spite of being willing to do so, she was never able to give me any more information on the subject.

The wonderful and terrible thing about your family tree being limited to just a single broken branch is that anything is possible. I was the descendant of the greatest hockey player of all time or the bastard child of the worst asshole, depending on my mood at any given moment. Sometimes I was even both at the same time. Move over, Schrödinger's cat.

I don't even know my real surname. That's weird too. I'm linked by blood and a mystery name to a whole bunch of strangers. It's kind of like having a huge brood of siblings but being the only one not to know anything about it. At the same time, it forces me to operate within a closed circuit. Everything stops with me. I don't know where I came from, and I have nothing to leave behind. A broken branch at the foot of a dead tree. You can't get freer than that.

Sometimes I find myself in front of the mirror looking for his features. I wonder if I'd recognize him if I bumped into him. Has he got acne and a prominent chin like me? Is he a redhead, but nearly brown, not really red, like me? Is he thin—skinny—like I am? Whenever a stranger stares at me, I imagine it's an acquaintance of my father, startled by the resemblance. I used to hope someone would come up to me and tell me the whole story, tell me all the unbelievable adventures that had kept him away from me, against his will, this whole time. Sometimes I just thought he must be dead. It would have cleared up a lot of things.

And now I wish he was dead.

I grew up in foster families, plural. I went through families like I went through birthdays. Social workers too. Moves, changes in care arrangements, school transfers, rewritten intervention plans.

I never liked the foster families. Everyone always said they believed in me, but nobody actually believed what I said. Just one paradox among many. Of course I lied, but everybody lies. All the time. To themselves, to other people, to the government, and whoever else. Everyone does it, but when you're a ward of the state and you exceed your quota, you're done for, they don't let anything else get past. It's a spiral. A fib to cover up a lie that was covering up a fib, and ultimately you're covered up pretty well, but you sleep badly. Anyway, even when I told the truth nobody listened to me. I was a misunderstood child.

I threw myself into it anyway. Sometimes I even managed to convince myself. I was pretty confident. It's important to believe in yourself, especially when you're lying.

A social worker warned me once that little hypocrites like me always hit a wall. And someone else told me that you learn at the school of hard knocks. One way or another, I was destined for erudition.

I read everything I could get my hands on. People left me

alone when I was reading; reading is sacred. Children would finally ignore me and adults could get a moment of peace. I even read dictionaries. The same way I read poetry—by letting it infuse me, without understanding everything. I soaked up literature, which is still important to me today. I had a penchant for dictionaries of quotations. One day I'd like to write quotations. I really should look into how you go about publishing them.

So I used to read. On the bus, in my corner of the schoolyard, in all the houses I was dragged around, in the washrooms, and during sleepless nights. Kinda hazardous with a lighter. My whole childhood is imprinted with comics, novels, porn mags, and dictionaries. I'm a visual person.

They said I didn't understand everything because I'm dysphasic. Their fake diagnosis didn't impress me much. I don't always understand the meanings of words? People don't even know the meaning of life yet, so is it really that big a deal if the meaning of certain words escape me?

But ever since kindergarten I'd been parked in a class for people with learning difficulties. I guess the jerks just couldn't be bothered to teach me anything. Most of the teachers cared as little about my school results as they did about my depression. Classroom peace was their top priority. I enjoyed injecting a bit of atmosphere, which meant I often found myself in the corridor or the principal's office.

With hindsight, I can confirm that I developed my distinctive voice and handwriting thanks to all those lines I had to write.

I will stop talking in class. I will respect the teachers. I will not steal. I will not fight. I will not insult the bus driver again. I will not pull Ariane's hair. I will walk on the right side of the corridor. Weeks passed, then we started over in a different order: *I will not steal, I will walk on the right side of the corridor, I will not bite Ariane,* etc. This basic application of behaviourism had limited success.

As well as being given lines, I also got sent to the quiet room a lot. *The respite room, the transition room,* or *the reflection room,* depending on the institution. Seriously, the effort that went into naming these places was equalled only by the uselessness of all the cognitive-behavioural stuff the counsellors loved so much. In actual fact they were pretty cool places where the most interesting, the most streetwise, students hung out. For me, at least, they were the main places I could meet friends, and even criminal associates.

I say meet friends, but I've never had a real friend. Except for Denise, the version *with* hair. I think it's a trust thing. Friendship implies a certain amount of giving of oneself, and I haven't even got enough of me for myself, so I can't really give anything to others. I've always used and let myself be used as necessary. I think I'm too clever to have a friend. People are endlessly disappointing.

And I say criminal associates, but I've never extended myself very far in that particular field. A bit of dealing here, a bit of light robbery there, without really making any lasting alliances. Humans are egocentric. I could foresee that collaborating in a school setting might just land me with a load of snitches. I had a bigger vision. I aspired to the Russian mafia or, in a pinch, the Italian one. Not the bikers, they have no class.

Year in, year out, I continued my education collecting diagnoses and failures. I had so much experience repeating grades that I could have gone into teaching. French was okay, but I flunked all the other subjects without so much as lifting a finger. Even art. I made myself dope pipes out of clay, and I drew nothing but naked ladies. I was studying curves and perspective. Great geniuses are always misunderstood.

On the behaviour front, things always came back to *plenty of room for improvement* and I suffered the minor consequences of my so-called problematic actions. Until Grade 5, first week of school, end of third period, at 12:12 p.m. It's burned into my memory forever.

All my friends had left the classroom for lunch. I was hanging back, arranging my porn sketches neatly in my desk. I was amazed to realize that Pierre-Louis, the teacher, had forgotten me. He'd left with the students and now I was in charge.

I started rifling through backpacks and pencil cases. I stole a few superhero erasers, a granola bar, and a comic book. I wandered aimlessly, intoxicated by possibilities I could barely even grasp. I stuck boogers on the blackboard as well as on Ariane's stuff. I soon ran out of organic resources. I was kicking my heels when a slight creak roused me from my torpor. At the back of the classroom, Bushy, the guinea pig, was moving. We were only allowed to pet him when Mr. Pierre-Louis was there; that was a strict rule. He was very fat and pretty—the guinea pig, not Pierre-Louis. Burnt toffee and white in colour, if I remember correctly. We were absolutely forbidden to let him out of his cage for any reason.

I suffocated him very carefully, out of curiosity. My hand barely went all the way round his body; his head and his butt stuck out at each end of my fist. I felt him wriggling and struggling uselessly. His little claws, moving frantically, tickled the palm of my hand. I gripped more tightly. I heard a crack. Blood trickled from his mouth. His eyes were popping wildly out of his head. I exerted light pressure and some of his intestines slipped out of his anus. I jumped and let him drop back into the cage, in total agony.

Pierre-Louis, searching for me, came into the classroom and found me standing next to the cage, rather pale. He raced over to it without even looking at me. When he saw Bushy dying in his wood shavings, he swore, then swore again as he turned to me. I automatically thought of reporting him to the principal for his unacceptable language, but the seriousness of my own somewhat compromising circumstances persuaded me against it. Out of fear or some kind of self-protective instinct, I started bawling hot tears, but they didn't help. He grabbed me by the arm and dragged me to the principal's office, where the decision to permanently expel me was a great relief to the vast majority of the teachers.

And so I was moved to a different foster family, and I went to finish elementary school in a special class in yet another school. In this class there were no rodents. But there was Mrs. Dubois. Her first name was France, but we weren't allowed to use it. I doubt if anybody in the world called her by her first name. It was too personal. It was obvious that nobody loved this cold, strict bitch. The only reason she'd ended up in teaching was because they didn't want her in the army. With her broad shoulders and moustache, she was certainly a virile woman.

Everything had its place, and Mrs. Dubois kept records of every single lapse in order. In her utterly logical mind, full of grids, our names appeared with checkmarks for each of our bad deeds. She could tell me precisely the number of times I'd failed to put the board eraser back in the right place. Everything had to be clean and ready for use. She was always droning on about how if everyone did things as perfectly as she did, people would be a lot better off. Sure they would—better off dead.

Mrs. Dubois managed to create good class solidarity, based entirely on the hatred we felt for her. How many recesses did we spend dreaming up schemes for our revenge? How many clenched fists fantasized about smashing her face? Her dictatorial style was hated but effective. I finished my elementary schooling that same year, and left that little hell for special classes at high school.

2

RESOURCEFULNESS

My arrival at high school was brightened by a realization: the most important thing in hostile spaces is not to be the strongest but the craziest. This is well documented.

I wasn't particularly strong, but I soon learned to fight. You have to aim for the testicles, the solar plexus, or the eyes. Hit them where it hurts. But boxing is nothing, as Cassius Ali said. And he ought to know, having personally broken a ton of jaws. So boxing isn't the important part; it's everything else you bring to it. I always carried a weapon on me, and I kept a stone gripped in my fist to increase its power and impact.

In spite of these precautions, I still lost fights. Too many for my liking. It's not so bad though, apart from the after-effects; whatever doesn't kill us makes us stronger. And there's no doubt about it, I'm a strong man.

Knowledge is power, said Eazy-E, that famous singer from Compton. I knew I had to tend the secret garden of my brain. I kept up with my habits and my reading. I stole everything that looked interesting from the public library. I also tried shoplifting from bookstores, but the alarm went off more often there—so I also had plenty of chances to go for a run.

The first time I killed a cat, I was as surprised as he was. In fact, as surprised as she was, since it was a little molly cat called Mimine. Mimine was a pretty product of back-alley mating, her bastard coat cleverly mixing brown, black, and ginger. She was a full-fledged member of my foster family at the time, the Doucets. I would have been fifteen then; Mimine was three.

For several months, I'd been in the habit of torturing animals whenever I was frustrated. I must have been very frustrated on that particular day. The animal didn't survive the combination of centrifugal force and my bedroom door frame. It made an odd noise, soft and dry at the same time. I was sitting on the bed, still holding Mimine by the tail, when there was a creak on the stairs.

Robert was coming down. I panicked. I slid the cat under the duvet and stretched out on top of it. *What noise?* No, it wasn't me that had made that noise. No, I hadn't nailed anything to the wall. Yes, I was coming up for dinner. Robert, the debonair patriarch of this reasonably functional family, had his eye on me, the eye of the tiger. He couldn't manage without the cash that social services gave him for looking after me, but never stopped telling me he'd had it up to here with my crap and I was *this close* to being shown the door. I didn't particularly like his dump of a house, or the people who lived in it, but I was fed up with moving. I liked having my own room in the basement, away from everyone else. And above all, this was the first foster home that had the Super Écran channel. After midnight on Fridays, Super Écran was fantastic.

I had to get rid of the body.

As per usual at this house, I wasn't allowed to go out that Sunday. I rolled the corpse up in a towel and stashed it between the mattress and the box spring for the day, waiting for Monday morning. Part of the evening was taken up with searching for the missing cat. I was particularly energetic in my efforts. The family lingered in my room but without any luck.

Fortunately for me, I was already seriously into hip hop, and wore it proudly. My oversized pants meant I could attach Mimine, with the help of some duct tape, to my inner left thigh as I was leaving the house. The corpse's stiffness restricted my movement a fair bit, but I managed to walk more or less normally. Enough to eat, then leave the house, without being noticed. With my schoolbooks under my arm, I went down the street, cursing myself for having traded my backpack for a tab of LSD. My thigh had started itching and was getting worse by the minute. I'd pulled the tape too tight. My leg was completely numb. Although maybe it was better that way, since the fur tickled less. The bus ride went on forever, there were three of us in one seat and I couldn't discreetly scratch my crotch.

Once I'd made my careful way to school, I smoked my morning cigarette and then headed for the toilets. Sitting on the throne, Mimine's body across my knees, I waited for the bell to ring and the washrooms to empty out, then I concealed the proof of my crime in the garbage under a pile of dirty paper towels. I had to run to class. I needn't have bothered—the teacher was already writing me a detention slip.

It was an ordinary school day. Brainwashing, surging hormones, and putting up with a bit of intimidation that was immediately passed on to anyone smaller. I liked the bustling atmosphere, and I really liked the girls. In return, they didn't particularly like me. I had a bad reputation and was too mature for my age. I never managed to screw any of them. My sole forays into teenage sex took place hidden behind a rusty merry-go-round at the fair. But that girl was ugly and weird, so it doesn't really count. Sometimes I regret that I didn't know how to meet those nymphettes' expectations back then. I caught up later though.

Although Operation Camouflage was successful, Mimine's disappearance was still blamed on me. They argued that the cat had never run away before, that Robert had heard a door slamming the previous day, that I smoked in secret, and that I must have let her out when I came through the garage. They were accusing me without proof. This felt like a grave injustice. I kicked a hole in the wall to show my indignation. I was quickly moved to another foster family. This one had a dog.

They were an obese bunch, this family. I have nothing against obese people, but you have to be pretty pathetic to let your body get into such a state. Glands, my ass! As well as Daddy Fat and Mommy Fat, there was their daughter Jenny, who didn't want to be left behind. And she certainly never left anything behind on her plate. As for me, I made sure to always leave something, playing with my food, lifting forkfuls to my mouth only to put them back down on the plate. It drove those fatties crazy. I used to chuckle to myself under my downy moustache.

They all sweated copiously. But the weirdest part was that they all sweated from their cracks when they exerted themselves. Their distended skin gave them long cracks. I was constantly wiping the toilet seat down. Little pearls of sweat glistened all around the white plastic ring. Sometimes I forgot and sat down in their toxins. That shut down my will to live, never mind my urgent need to go.

Three other kids were placed with this moist family. All ballsy kids full of testosterone like me. We lived in the basement and kept ourselves busy altering our minds by any means possible. Obviously we could get hold of plenty of stuff at school and in the neighbourhood, but we were also pretty ingenious. For example, rather than just inhaling gas, we poured it into a metal can that we heated so it would give off fumes. We also mixed liquid paper with ground-up pills and snorted it. We watched the effects of these mixtures on each other's faces. The bulk of our free time was dedicated to research, buying psychotropic substances, and developing ways to use them. The foster family had frying, we had initiative.

When we weren't stealing from each other, we basement musketeers got along well. Even with Benjamin, our whipping boy. A whipping boy is good for group dynamics. He was the gang's outlet. I lived there with something like stability for a while.

We slept two to a room. I shared my privacy with Steve, a Haitian two years older than me. He had a huge cock, a truly massive penis. I'm not saying that to be racist, black people are very well hung. It's a genetic thing.

Steve and I burned with the same passion for hip hop and we wrote a few rap songs together. We had the chemistry, the talent, and the attitude too. All we needed was a musician to set it to a beat and a manager to launch the product. We already had a name: Sons of the Street. It was good. Our concept was all ready to go; we'd always wear white and black, and shoot videos in black and white. Him in white, me in black. A real mix of genres. We were even going to be famous in France, but a few months later social services took Steve to a secure unit.

Steve and I were the black sheep in this foster family. People came down hard on us every chance they got. Especially when we beat up Benjamin, the mentally ill kid. They banged on about how it was unacceptable, but they all refused to understand that we beat him up because he was an asshole, not because he was mentally ill. They aren't mutually exclusive. We didn't give a fuck if he was bipolar, the problem was that he was intrusive, he ratted on us, and stole from us. You can be mentally ill and still be an asshole.

They'd had us in their sights ever since Benjamin's last

thrashing. Steve was sent back to the centre not long after that. He'd casually threatened the head of the family with a butter knife. A butter knife just isn't that dangerous. The mother panicked and jumped out the first-floor window, tearing her meniscus. In Steve's defence, I should point out that he did call an ambulance. I never saw him again, it was a shame. At least I had the room to myself and could masturbate whenever I felt like it. Every cloud has a silver lining.

Speaking of which, the size of my pants had several advantages. As well as being able to carry dead cats and steal objects of considerable size, I discovered that I could fondle myself without attracting too much attention. I'd gone to the trouble of poking holes in the bottoms of my pockets, having developed an ambidextrous technique. Success depended on fine motor skills and dexterity. In practical terms, you just had to repeatedly pinch the glans, without any back and forth that might arouse suspicion. I particularly enjoyed doing it during my appointments with the school psychologist.

Claudia's professionalism turned on all the guys, as-yet-undecideds, and burgeoning lesbians in the school. She owned a collection of suits, each one more fitted than the last. Very classy and top of the line. I liked the beige suit best. It outlined the curve of her breasts beautifully, and the skirt revealed enough thigh to fuel my developing pubescent imagination.

My personalized intervention plan dictated that I had to meet with her every two weeks. I discovered I could increase the frequency of these meetings by inventing existential worries or by revealing the pithy details of my life. Like the story about Mimine the cat, for example. Her dramatic intensity when I fed her unhealthy curiosity for all the details was exciting. It made her feel important, and maybe she imagined that she was something of a help to me.

I never ejaculated in her office. Back then I wasn't very

good at controlling my facial spasms. Having an orgasm always made my face twist up. I practised in front of a mirror but I never managed to stay completely stoic. It was a philosophical matter. I didn't want anything whatsoever to interrupt our appointments, and I didn't want to end up forced to keep my hands on my knees. So I stopped by the washrooms before going to art lessons, my body and spirit light.

Claudia inhabited my imagination for several years—seven, to be precise. She provided the inspiration for my solitary caresses until the day I bumped into her under the cruel neon lights of a grocery store. Time had assaulted her face. Her migratory breasts were heading south. And not even the same south as each other. One of them seemed to be stretching her blouse in a southeasterly direction. She was suffering from a mammary strabismus. It's pretty common in women who don't have the money to get implants. I pretended I didn't recognize her. She did the same thing. I left the store without even buying my Cap'n Crunch, abandoning my destroyed fantasy in the cereal aisle.

After two years with the chubster family—a record—I had to move again. My sense of initiative and my interest in science were not appreciated. Along with the other foster kids in the house, I'd started testing psychoactive substances on Rocket, the family beagle. It wasn't a big deal or even that dangerous. We didn't have the means to give him the amounts we took ourselves, but we often chipped in so that he could join us. One PCP-fuelled Saturday night, we chipped in a bit too much. Rocket got way too stoned.

Before we took it ourselves, we'd all put some of our precious powder in his water. We soon realized that for once the drug hadn't been cut with anything. The evening was unfolding well and we were sharing a nice little high. Especially Benjamin, who stared fascinated at Rocket, as he gnawed his paws passionately. Unfortunately for us, the family returned earlier than expected from their trip to the movies. We were still in the basement living room, standing round the dog and tormenting him. When he saw his owners, he tried to get up to go over to them, but he could only manage to crawl on his side, dragging the living room rug under his flank. Rocket seemed to have an issue with the concept of gravity that evening.

Daddy Double-Fat judged the situation to be extremely serious, correctly diagnosed that we were totally wasted, and called an emergency social worker. I magnanimously took the fall. As the oldest, and the most experienced in sudden relocations, I assured the social jerker they'd called to the rescue that since I'd organized the little party, I understood I'd have to be the one to hit the road. As I left, I shot one last look at Rocket, who was squinting in my direction.

At sixteen, I'd already burned through all the foster families in the region and they wanted to get me out of the group homes as quickly as possible. I harmed the progress of the other kids in a closed unit. If those little shits hadn't disturbed my serenity, I wouldn't have wrecked their facial symmetry. Everything's always a question of viewpoint. Or of fists in the gob. They beat us round the head with ideas of respect and listening but it was pointless; there are few arguments as effective as a knuckle sandwich for getting a message across. The problem was that this opinion was shared by several other youths in my unit. We dealt out these arguments to each other for anything and nothing. Things were tense. I think we were fond of each other even if we did often hurt each other. Punching is human contact, after all.

I've heard that counsellors were assigned to our unit as punishment. This led to a bad atmosphere: they sent us the worst people, who rolled up full of prejudices toward us. You should never judge a man until you've limped along in his prosthetics.

I remember one worker in particular, Aïcha. She humiliated me in front of everybody one evening during cleanup. It was her way of punishing me. She suspected me—correctly—of having hidden her car keys for several hours one Monday morning when I was feeling playful. But that's no excuse. She let the other guys in the unit hear that she'd caught me crying. I don't do crying. Although I'm normally quick-witted, I didn't reply to her right then.

I had the chance to get my revenge later.

3

INDEPENDENCE

When I was seventeen, it was decided that I could live in an apartment with partial supervision, near the administrative offices of the youth centre. They put me into a special program preparing me for a life of total independence, where I learned to forget how to plan a budget. Then they opened a savings account in which I didn't save anything. They also gave me group cooking lessons. Naturally I brought my own spices from time to time. I was nearly eighteen when they took me to look for an apartment, just outside downtown.

After four viewings, I was pretty sick of the whole thing, and ready to sign the first lease put in front of me. Unfortunately, the counsellor who came with me was a real keener. A tall gorgeous babe in full makeup and wearing leatherette boots. The kind who lingers in your mind after lights out.

She considered the proportions of the rooms, explained to me how to let the light in and a whole whack of other useless things. I can't even imagine how many hours she'd wasted watching interior-design shows. Poor girl, if she'd known the upkeep I was going to devote to my abode, she'd have let me sign for the storeroom of some Cambodian buffet. We eventually agreed on a one-bedroom near the centre and a grocery store. One thirty-seven Maple Street, apartment 4. I had some happy times there. And it was in this hovel that I owned my first cat, Princess.

I celebrated my eighteenth birthday by spending half of my first welfare cheque on a tattoo. For humans—unlike cattle—marking your body is a sign of liberty. I'd learned this during my hours online. I needed something original, something unique that really represented me. I got a tattoo of a big Chinese character on the back of my neck. *Strength*. That's what the tattoo meant. It was impressive.

When I'm inside, I'll get one whole arm and part of my back tattooed. I'll also get the prisoners' star on my hand, between my thumb and index finger.

I was getting through a lot of marijuana and video games in that period of my life. It's a very effective combination for busting boredom, but it does do a bit of a number on productivity. I was into all forms of rebellion and prided myself on screwing society. Back then I didn't understand that society was screwing me back just as hard.

I wasn't suffering much from being an inactive member of the system and I managed to convince my supervisor that my attempts to look for a job were totally pointless. I sabotaged interviews. I knew I was worth more than they had to offer me. I was too young to be given a management position, so I always had to apply for the assistant positions. *Working a loser job, you'll stay a loser* was one of my philosophies. All I had to do was wait for the opportunity to start straight in as a manager or owner. I felt I had the potential already.

I could smoke two or three grams of weed and still manage to devote eight or nine hours a day to my game console. Most people, narrow-minded and uncultivated, don't see the concrete applications and the competences you develop during days spent hammering away with a joystick. For me, however, it was valuable. I got a good grounding in English, sharpened my sense of strategy, and it helped me manage my stress whenever I couldn't get my hands on Princess.

In particular, I improved my skills as a shooter thanks to my favourite war games. I should point out that I also practised with a BB gun that I'd exchanged, for nothing, with a young guy in the neighbourhood. I was teaching myself to shoot birds and squirrels perched on the electrical wires outside my window. I rarely managed to kill one, but often hit them. They got away, or fell off the cable onto the sidewalk. I'd have made an excellent marksman in the army. I've thought about doing that. I have the strength of character and warrior spirit you need for large-scale missions.

I don't think I was addicted, but I smoked my first joint in the morning, before breakfast, to spark my appetite. The days didn't seem so long. I rented games or I went to invest in the slot machines at Chez Manon, the fancy bar conveniently located at the corner of the street.

I couldn't say whether I won more than I lost in my first years of playing, but one thing is certain: I learned to read the machine, to decode the algorithm for getting the big bucks. Except that most of the machines were rigged or responded badly to my strategy. My welfare money was rapidly returned to the state or was disbursed among local traders. I used to make it to the end of the month by stealing bikes and running a few nice little scams.

I liked adult life. I accepted my responsibilities; I was free from the yoke of youth protection. The only thing left was to find my mother and then life would be good.

Life is shit. Those organizations that help reunite you with people couldn't do anything for me. I hadn't been adopted. *Of course I wasn't adopted, I have a mother! She didn't abandon me, I was ripped from her arms!* They couldn't help me with the process, I would absolutely have to go through social services.

And social services told me they'd lost track of her. When it was time to ruin our lives and break up our family, those assholes didn't have any trouble keeping track of us then! I often lost my temper with them on the phone. In their offices too. Security had to intervene.

One time an employee dared to tell me that he'd looked extensively through my file and he'd come to the conclusion that I'd be better off abandoning my search and finding myself a different parent figure. I threw his stapler at his head. He was so condescending—refused to make an official complaint, but banned me from entering the building. At last I knew the truth. I couldn't count on the system for getting me back in touch with Mama. You are never better served than by yourself.

I was using more and more, so I was stealing to match. It was my way of getting revenge, at least for now. While I waited to gather the necessary weapons. I didn't want to help social services by becoming the good little statistic they were after. By messing myself up, I screwed them over too.

Sometimes I filled my need to get back at them by vandalizing their buildings. On a more personal level, I smeared crap on Aïcha's car every two months. Give or take. Poor Aïcha, she hadn't known who she was dealing with. Jesus forgives, I get revenge. It was a bad idea to find me an apartment near the centre.

I was a suspect. Two investigators came to the apartment. I'd read Mario Puzo and watched the investigations on the crime channels. I understood their techniques and I knew they had nothing on me. They were hardly going to take DNA samples from shit.

During the interrogation, one of the policemen was staring at me for ages. It was embarrassing. For him in particular; he looked like an imbecile. As for me, I was stressed, as I usually am when there are cops, but I was relieved to wiggle out of it. At the end of the intimidation session, he hissed between his clenched teeth, *You have to be a real bastard to do that.*

People are bastards and life's a bitch. *You're right, Mr. Policeman.*

I left Aïcha in peace. Her car no longer had anything to fear. And Princess no longer had to wonder why her turds were disappearing from her litter box.

4

MATURITY

I'm a lucky man. Although I think we make our own luck, I feel the presence of a superior power. It watches over me and gives a little wink now and then. Like the evening of my twenty-first birthday. Having failed to get hold of anyone who wanted to go out, I decided to celebrate, going it alone but going big.

Marie-Josée was filling in for Manon at the bar. I drank several strong shots with her and she let me play one of my favourite albums. She warned me she'd have to turn it off if someone came in. The usual customers weren't huge gangsta rap fans. But the bar didn't usually have any customers, so we listened to the whole album.

An alignment of the stars, the music, and my pro player skills allowed me to extract two hundred and eighty-four dollars from the state-owned machine. The bells rang and paid out at last. I'd invested close to two hundred dollars upfront, but it still worked out to a nice profit. Enough to excite Marie-Josée, who brought out a good amount of gin and a few drops of tonic. Wealth has been turning women on since the dawn of time. It's well documented.

We started heavy petting in the taxi, going off to track down some amphetamines and cocaine to spice up the night. Marie-Josée stared into the rear-view mirror while she rubbed my cock. The driver must have been pretty jealous. It got me a bit too aroused and I ejaculated in my pants.

Once we'd got to her place, we resumed our frolicking in the shower. In bright light she was less beautiful. She was skinny and clung on to me without touching the floor. Very acrobatic. I beat my taxi performance by a good three minutes. We showered and then sat in the kitchen chain-smoking.

I wanted to buy some time to recover. I started to tell her about my life, all my moves and my ambitions as a rapper. I explained to her that I wanted to find my mother along the way, when I was all set up. She was touched. So was I. She cried between two puffs of freebase. She could identify with that, she said. She had three children, placed in a foster home for the time being. But she was following a voluntary program and was convinced she'd get them back soon. Everything's a question of confidence. Always.

She tried to take me in her mouth, but I was too high to appreciate it, so we stayed at the confidences stage until the wee hours. When the other renters in the building began to move around, we tried to sleep. No luck. Nothing's more effective than the early birds and workers for making creatures of the night feel guilty. It's a reality check into the boards.

Without missing a beat, Marie-Josée dove like an Olympic athlete into anxiety. She was trembling with fear that she'd be fired for having closed the bar early. She was scared of seeing a social worker show up. She'd sworn to herself that she'd never smoke that shit again. I cut it and took over, out of compassion. I talked without stopping to distract her, whispering so that nobody in the building would hear me. We were barely listening to each other. Between two muttered words we could hear the grinding of our teeth. Hers were yellow. Around ten, I thought she was finally going to fall asleep, but she suddenly came out with, *What was your mother's name?*

Why?

No reason, just tell me what her name was.

My mother's name is Marie-Madeleine Fontaine.

I didn't even have enough money to take the bus. I walked half-way across town mumbling a new chorus.

I've got nothing to lose!
I can leave you in your blood
Or in your shit
Nothing nothing nothing to lose!

I had to find a musician and a record label as soon as possible, I was losing vast sums. Ever since I got my start with Steve, I'd never stopped. I was constantly improving. I had ideas, rhymes, and concepts that would transform the industry. I even considered making my career in the United States. That's where it all happens.

I only had six cigarettes left for the day. I was going to have to space them out. I already had a cough deeper than a coal mine, so this time of shortage could only be good for my health. I told myself I'd known worse. I also recalled some Buddhist thoughts picked up from magazines. *Life is suffering. Nothing lasts. Everything is ephemeral.* He developed the whole concept of relativity, old Buddha.

Twelve hours earlier I'd had the night in front of me and nearly three hundred dollars in my pocket. I no longer had any of that, but I had a new notch on the bedpost and the proof that my gambling strategies had turned out to be profitable. Which wasn't nearly enough to convince Mr. Paul, the owner of the filthy building I lived in. He had a habit of threatening to call the rental board every time we saw each other, but this time he was waiting for me, *and my foot is twitching*. He could stick his twitchy foot up his ass.

Planted in front of my apartment door, ready to take root if necessary, he swore he wouldn't budge from there until I paid him. I could hear Princess yowling behind the door. My cat hadn't eaten for two days. And yet again I'd forgotten to steal her some sausages. I reckoned that Princess's needs were a good enough argument for letting me in. I argued, but then, remembering that the reed doesn't bend for anybody, I wisely said, *Alright, champ, I'll go and get some money.*

An evil smile was the only answer from the fat bourgeois.

Stay right there, I'll be back.

I'm not moving until I have at least one month's rent in my hands.

That's the idea, don't move at all!

I went out through the main door and walked along the building. Grabbing the balcony, I managed to haul myself up to my second-floor apartment. I'd had to force the window open one evening when I'd forgotten my key. Mr. Paul hadn't felt any urgent need to repair it.

As soon as I set foot in the apartment, Princess started mewing her head off. *Shh, sshh.* I pretended to throw her a piece of food. She looked for it hungrily. That calmed her down. I headed for the bedroom, picked up the sports bag I never used, and stuffed it with every valuable thing I had in the place. My console and games, a bit of tequila, some albums, some clean and dirty clothes, stroke mags, and rolling papers.

My good bourgeois must have heard me. The noise of his keys alerted me just in time. I pushed the couch against the door and sat on it, bursting into laughter.

Now who's the sucker, Mr. Paul? If you give me one more week to pay the rent, I'll let you in, okay?

He made a real racket tearing down the stairs. I could

barely hear the threats he left swirling in his wake. *I'm going to call the police! You're out! Out! Never again...* I guess he was refusing my offer.

Youth services would have problems placing anyone else in that building. I felt a certain amount of pride at the thought that he'd have to contact them to find me or to get reimbursed. Even if they had no more legal obligation concerning me, I'd managed to cause them some trouble. *Screw you, screw landlords, and screw rent. Freedom!*

Screw the police too, but the less I saw of them the better. So I had to leg it. Mr. Paul always meant what he said.. He'd make good on his threats. While I was getting ready to climb over the balcony railing, Princess came out and started weaving figure eights around my legs, meowing louder than ever. I felt a pang in my heart. I couldn't leave her there. I couldn't take her with me either. I had to make a devastating but necessary decision. I could understand parents who murder their children out of love, to protect them.

I killed two birds with one stone. Princess wouldn't be abandoned, and Mr. Paul would know what kind of cloth I was cut from. I stuck a steak knife in Princess's neck to cut her head off. It's harder to decapitate a cat than you might think. She struggled. A geyser of blood spurted out and stained my pants. Furious, I stabbed the knife in her back two or three times, then swung her against the entrance door, spattering the old grey carpet in the process. Even today, I can't help laughing when I imagine Mr. Paul's face.

Marie-Josée refused to let me stay at her place. Youth services might show up at any moment. If they discovered a man in her life or in her apartment that they hadn't been notified of, it could compromise her children's return. I bargained hard to spend the afternoon there at least. Just a bit of time to get myself organized and find somewhere to go.

We fucked, but I didn't feel her heart was in it. It was mechanical, disembodied. She was more into it with a massive dose of stimulants in her blood, but we were totally wrecked. It has to be said that in the light of day, with a sleepless night behind me, she lost a lot of what little charm she'd had.

We smoked my last cigarettes while we looked for somewhere for me to live. I wanted nothing to do with community resources. The landlord would definitely have got the police on the case. It was the first place they'd check.

Paranoid, Marie-Josée asked why the police wanted to find me. She grimaced, disturbed, when I told her about Princess. I felt her judgment. I hate that. I burst out laughing and assured her it was a joke, but the blood on my pants gave me away. I fed her a tale about some meat I'd wanted to get from the fridge. I don't think I got myself out of it too badly.

People's crass hypocrisy exasperates me. *Oh no, he killed a cat!* So what, for fuck's sake? We stuff our faces with dead animals all year long. Hundreds of them. Thousands. Tens of thousands during a lifetime. And of course tons of them are tortured during the process, raised in disgusting conditions, separated from their mothers and force-fed before being assassinated to feed human slugs. And I'm supposed to feel guilty about having killed my own cat, that I brought up and loved? I lit my last cigarette and insisted on spending the evening and the coming night at Marie-Josée's. But the mood had changed.

She jumped up, spluttering that she had an idea. She grabbed the phone, and it must have taken her three tries to dial the right number, she was trembling so much. Fear or withdrawal, maybe both. She mumbled as she twirled one of her blond locks around her fingers, mixed with a good amount of brown regrowth. Relief was written all over her face when she hung up.

*My aunt Nicole is coming to pick you up. She has a house in
Saint-Agapit and rents out rooms. She's agreed to spot you two weeks
until your cheque arrives. She's cool, you'll see, Nicole is supercool.*

I felt like she was getting rid of me. She even asked me
to not show up at her place without warning. I did actually
need an address to get my social security cheque sent to. Aunt
Nicole's address would do the trick. Marie-Josée disappointed
me with the smallness of her sorrow. While we waited we made
love anyway.

She rushed through the introductions and let me leave
without even a kiss, nothing. I'd told her my whole life story. I
thought it was more serious, the two of us. But I didn't give a shit.
At the end of the day she was too skinny and a bit of an idiot.

5

ADAPTABILITY

The bedroom was small and damp. The whole basement smelled of old wet wood. It wasn't unbearable, but it still showed the place was prone to mould. But unlike the wood, I didn't plan on sitting around here rotting for long. Especially as I'd forgotten to refill my inhaler prescription. I was already spitting up my lungs, and some blood, when I got up. It wasn't as bad if I woke up after noon. *The bird who gets up catches the worm*, as Shakespeare, a European author, said.

Leaving the capital for such a tiny village was disorienting. I noticed a lack of stores and things to do. It was a problem. I'd borrowed enough money from Aunt Nicole to buy up the local dealer's entire amphetamine stock, but I was seriously bored. I needed to get hold of a computer to feed my passions, both pornography and reading, and soon. I could also use it to get back in touch with the world and, eventually, with a nice fat cash cow.

I roamed the fields, surveying the houses. I kept a respectable distance back from residences. Shadow was my friend. After an hour of scouting, I stumbled across the ideal place. All the lights were off, no vehicle in the drive, no dog in the yard. I moved closer and my enthusiasm grew. A nice lower-middle-class bungalow with no alarm system. It's always easier to rob poor people, the government will confirm that. No doubt I'd find a laptop and some bottles of alcohol. Screwdriver, plastic frame, pressure, window open, go in, bingo! I didn't even need my flashlight. The full moon was enough to light up the place. It was a sign.

A good looter knows how to find the treasure in five minutes, tops. I did the whole thing in four. Three Coors Light in the fridge. What kind of imbecile tries to get drunk on four per cent alcohol? You'd drown first. An old PlayStation console in the living room. Not worth much, but easy to sell. In the main bedroom, a handful of jewellery and a basket of dirty laundry.

I extracted four G-strings from the basket and pressed them to my face. This little lady had had some long workdays. The smell was strong and persistent. I stuffed the swag in my pocket and continued exploring.

I sensed movement in the basement as soon as I set foot on the stairs. The flashlight, an industrial one, would do. I got it out of my bag, grasped the long steel tube, and leapt the last few steps. If there was a troublemaker in the cellar, I'd need to overpower him before he could call the police.

It was a cat, of course. I didn't track it down, but there were two litter boxes next to the dryer. Bastard cat. I pissed over its turds just to annoy it. I also pissed in the open washer. There was a big load of whites waiting. I laughed. I'm easily entertained.

I didn't find my much-wanted laptop, but I could make do with an old Pentium tower and flat screen. It was hard to carry, but I wouldn't attract too much attention going back through the fields.

I discovered love on a dating site. I met—virtually—an unbelievable number of extremely rude women who stopped writing to me for absolutely no reason. I'm a persistent man. I got back in touch, as determined as an obese person at a buffet. Finding love was practically a full-time job. I spent days on those sites looking for that precious stone. Okay, semi-precious. No need to fool ourselves, there's a ton of lard-asses and desperate people exposing themselves on there. It had taken me dozens of hours, and nearly as many identity changes, but I'd finally made it.

I felt too isolated in my little bedroom at the bottom of the little house in the little village. Me, I think big.

After we'd lived together for a month, Aunt Nicole turned out to be far less cool than advertised. I always had to pick up after myself and wash my own dishes. At least she let me be in charge of cleaning my own room, which I never did. I also stretched out the rent a little, telling myself I'd fly by night one of these evenings. Love arrived just in time.

When I met Audrey, my profile said I was an engineer; I could clarify later that I was an engineer looking for work. I was actually planning to study engineering and then look for work in the field afterwards. So it wasn't entirely dishonest.

Audrey was a nurse, but most importantly she was blessed with enormous breasts. Women's chests reveal a lot about their personality. I've surveyed a lot of data on discussion forums to back up this theory. Audrey proved that women with a big chest tend to be generous and shy. For me, these are the top two important qualities. Massive boobs are the third and fourth. Incidentally, Audrey had curly red hair but no freckles.

Right from our first date I knew it was the start of a passionate affair. She was looking for a serious relationship, spent a lot of time playing sports, and loved animals, just like me. She worked nights in a hospital emergency department. It was perfect, since I always got up around noon, so I could meet up with her at the end of the day and spend my evenings at her place. Audrey came to pick me up in the village and drove me to the capital. I always arranged to meet her in front of the nicest beautiful house in Saint-Agapit.

Audrey was pretty bad at cooking, but she had a beautiful apartment high up, with views plunging down over the town. I don't know why, but nothing made me feel more rich and powerful than standing by that window. I dominated the capital. With some decent rocket launchers and a few cobalt machine guns, I could have done some serious damage. Audrey was clueless about weapons and video games. Women rarely get good at these things.

Her cats were not as well brought up as Princess; they were constantly climbing onto the counters. I swept them off with the back of my hand whenever Audrey's back was turned. If she was in another room I gave them a good thump.

Audrey also liked me to hit her, take her from behind, bite and insult her, within the limits of consensual politeness. She was very sexual for a nurse. She worked out all the stress of hemorrhages, resuscitations, and other hospital crises by offering herself up like that, her head stuffed into the pillow. She truly was an amazing woman.

I'm an intense man. I think a lot. My way of life forces me to be resourceful, creative, and practical. I welcome every chance to save a bit of time. Even when it comes to sex. Women who fuck like it's a sport, who throw themselves into it violently, are perfect for me. There's nothing duller than endless candlelit massage sessions. I like women who know what they want, especially when it's the same thing I want.

I was ready to move in after a few dates, but I found she was becoming more distant as the relationship matured. The devil is in the detail. The way she looked at me and how often she didn't, her remarks about my personal hygiene, some little note she left for me. She didn't even have time to read my poems anymore. And yet I'm a great poet. She still hadn't introduced me to her parents, or to her friends. She no longer listened so devotedly when I told her about the things I was doing to find my mother.

After two weekends when she *absolutely* couldn't get away, I was seriously having doubts. So naturally I started spying on her. I had lots of time to analyze every possible infidelity scenario. Hitching from Saint-Agapit to Quebec City when you're as big as me isn't easy, it can take a while. Those good Samaritan fuckers have got better things to do than help a man get his love life straightened out.

Often her car wasn't there. They said she was unavailable when I phoned the hospital, no matter what time I called. I went there faking a sprain. Audrey threw a little tantrum. She didn't want to see me. I had no business being there. She would call me when she wanted to get in touch. It was a complete load of crap. Didn't I have the right to be injured like everyone else?

We'd been dating for three weeks. That's not nothing. I had the right to know what was going on. Thanks to the personal information she'd shared with me, I was able to answer the security questions for her email and change her password in the process.

I don't know what I was expecting. The worst, I guess. It was worse than the worst. The amphetamine I'd swallowed before embarking on this archaeological enterprise was astonishingly good. I spent all night researching. I must have read close to two thousand archived messages. For a self-taught guy, I'm pretty good at psychoanalysis. I filled out her psychological profile with numerous details. I knew her better than she knew herself.

I discovered the emails she and her ex had written to each other during the two years they'd been together. It was kitten this and pussycat that, love letters as long as your arm, and promises straight out of the sappiest romance novel. Page after page of declarations of love. Page after page she'd never written to me.

I felt profoundly betrayed. Deep down, I'm a sensitive guy. She loved Gregory, or had loved him, more than me, that was obvious, and it was unacceptable. She'd cheated on me in some way. In the worst way. She'd given herself to me when she was no longer hers to give. Being unfaithful sexually is one thing, but infidelity of the heart is unspeakably disgraceful. I wrote down that sentence, it's worthy of Oscar Wilde—or Orson Welles, I get them mixed up.

I'd decided to kidnap her cats. The following week, on Thursday evening, during her shift at work. I'd written her a letter explaining my grief, setting out my reproaches. I'd weighed my words carefully. The note was in no way hysterical. She wasn't investing in the relationship as she should have done and as she'd led me to hope during our first exchanges on Network Contact. Above all, she was offering me a second-hand love, a thrift-store passion, in which I was only useful for filling the void left by her wonderful Gregory.

As a postscript, I explained that I was taking her cats because she cared about them more than she cared about me, until she decided to put more effort in and not contact Gregory anymore. I left the letter under the key to her apartment, which I was leaving at the same time. I'd had a copy cut that morning. You can never be too prepared.

I only found one of the cats, Ti-Gris. The other one must have been hiding under the furniture. Too bad, but then again so much the better: one hostage is easier to carry than two.

Ti-Gris was overexcited and threw up on the passenger seat of Nicole's Corolla, which I'd convinced her to lend me by pleading exceptional circumstances. My ex's cats were very badly brought up. Especially Ti-Gris. And then, as I was shoving his face in it to teach him a lesson, he scratched my arm. That did it; I grabbed him by the scruff of his neck and threw him out the window onto the highway. In the rear-view mirror I watched him roll and bang into a guardrail. I immediately felt a huge relief, and a great emptiness as well. I dithered for a bit about whether to go back and get the other hostage.

I was smoking one cigarette after another, driving along the 276, when my phone started vibrating with Audrey's first calls. She was already home. Maybe a neighbour had told her about my visit. I was worried about her reaction. I didn't know how to tell her that Ti-Gris had escaped. I decided to let my voice mail handle the situation.

In the end, the content of Audrey's messages showed me she was too emotional to get involved in a serious relationship. She shouted at my voice mail and threatened me with all kinds of bad things, in particular reporting me to the police. It was clearly exaggeration and I never replied to her. It's better to let a fire die out than to suffocate it with dead wood.

I still sometimes feel sorry for myself or stroke myself when I think of Audrey. It might have been a brief love, but it was love all the same.

6

HOPE

've found your mother, I really have. Marie-Josée's gravelly voice reminded me of her thin body and soft tongue.

Be careful what you say, Marie-Jo.

I'm totally serious, I've done some research and I've found her. You were right, she's in the Eastern Townships. Her aunt Nicole, who'd handed me the telephone, was watching my reactions out of the corner of her eye. She never came down to the basement normally. I lit a cigarette without noticing there was already one burning in the ashtray.

First off, why are you meddling in this?

I'm not meddling in anything, you're the one who said you'd always promised yourself you'd find her. I thought it was sweet. I just wanted to help you.

Nicole turned on the television for show, wedged hypocritically in the least comfortable corner of the couch to get a good angle, as much on me as on the conversation.

You didn't even want to see me again. You dump me and then you go poking around in my life?

Are you paranoid or what? You're the one who never got in touch. I haven't seen you at the bar for a month. You're the one who's sulking.

Nicole couldn't keep up the pretence, she turned to face me and lowered the volume on the TV. This was something of major interest. I stood up and went to my bedroom to continue the conversation. The volume of *La Poule aux oeufs d'or* went up dramatically, to a level that could only signal annoyance.

How did you find my mother? Social services always told me that that kind of information is confidential, that they couldn't give it to me.

You think I called social services? I just did some Google-stalking, which led me to Canada 411. Marie-Madeleines are pretty few and far between. The only one I've found is in the Eastern Townships. There's no such thing as coincidence. It's your mother. You have to go and find her.

It was too stupid for me to have thought of it myself.

When you repeatedly commit suicide, you end up dying. That's what I used to tell myself, that she had to be dead, her as well. Like my father. It was reassuring to say that to myself regularly. She wasn't suffering anymore, she'd left for good and I was alone. But knowing that she was alive, in the Eastern Townships, surely hopeful of finding me and picking up our family life where we left off, was overwhelming.

She'd probably tried to find me when I turned eighteen. The social workers wanted to protect me from her, just like they claimed when I was younger. Those dirty hell rats. I immediately put everyone whose name I could remember on my revenge list. Along with some of the foster parents, some jerks who'd stabbed me in the back, and some fuckers who'd unfairly turned me down, they'd be in good company.

Poor Mama. She must have made as much effort as I had to celebrate our reunion. Maybe she'd managed to get my contact details in the last few weeks. She might even have gone to my apartment. I hoped Mr. Paul hadn't told her what I'd done to Princess, that might give her a bad impression of me. I'd be able to explain it to her, though. She'd understand.

Twelve forty-six Prospect Street, Sherbrooke J1J 1J4. I even had the phone number: 819-555-4412. When I was a teenager, I was constantly bugging the social workers to find out this information. To the point of exhaustion—theirs too. And in the end it was some coked-up barmaid who'd given me the grail.

I wrote the information down on three different scraps of paper. I wanted to be sure I wouldn't lose it. I knew it all off by heart in less than a day anyway. I smoked and panted all week long. I was struggling to contain my joy. It stopped me from sleeping, suppressed my appetite, and chipped my nails. I masturbated even more than usual, and usual was already quite a lot. I got up to four times a day, sometimes five. Luckily I had my zinc cream. The foreskin soon gets irritated and the skin on the head splits when you call on it too often. I'd also started stuttering again. There's no doubt about it, I was very happy.

I was going to find my mother.

First of all I needed to rustle up some cash for the bus. I couldn't hitchhike at night with my bag full of objects of peculiar origins. The end justifies the means: I swallowed two amphetamines and got ready for a night of shopping in the country.

I made sure to fill my big canvas bag before setting out on this new quest. I stuffed everything I owned inside—in case I had to leave that same night. That way I could grab my things and hide out near the bus stop, get on the first one that came along, and, once morning came, start my new life. Clothes, porn mags, and cigarettes. All the essentials.

My jaw was working by itself. That was a good sign, the pills were getting into my bloodstream. My nerves were soaking up energy. The night would be lucrative, I could feel it. I pulled on my boots and my black hoodie, shoved my gloves and the screwdriver to the bottom of my pockets.

As soon as I heard Nicole's bed creak, right over my head, I pulled myself out through the window, went along the fence, and slipped into the woods behind the house. I lit a cigarette. *The night is mine*, as Al Pacino might have shouted, but I couldn't draw attention to myself. I rejoiced in silence. You can't imagine the power of the prowler, the freedom and euphoria that mingle in the heart of someone who's ready for anything. I got drunk on these thoughts as I moved through the backyards, looking for someplace that suited my needs. Time was passing and I wasn't finding anything. The night was turning out to be chilly. I'm not a wimp, but I was afraid of catching a cold.

Just as I was on the verge of getting discouraged, the idea of a holdup came to me. There's rarely any hard cash in houses. Unless it's jars of coins that are really heavy and really annoying. And I couldn't burden myself with things that I'd need to fence. I wanted to hit the road as soon as possible. Yes, what I needed was the contents of a cash drawer. I looked at the time and—like a sign from heaven!—the village convenience store would be closing in twenty minutes. All the day's takings were sitting waiting for me.

I pushed my hood down, went back to the road, and picked up the pace. It would be moronic to get there too late. A rusty pickup skimmed past me. It's a poor village, but still, they really ought to put in sidewalks. It's dangerous for honest citizens. The truck turned into the parking lot of the store, a hundred metres ahead, but did a U-turn right away. It was coming back toward me. I wrapped my fist around the screwdriver in my pocket when the pickup slowed down alongside me.

Excuse me, I'm trying to find an address but my GPS is broken. Can you help me? The guy seemed harmless, with his overly neat little goatee. He had to be gay.

I crossed the road. Through the open window he held out his phone to me. I didn't have time to check whether his directions were right. The second bastard must have been moving along the truck as I was crossing the road. I barely saw him pop up in my field of vision. A big ape with his arms raised. I didn't see it at the time, but he must have been armed with a stick or a club.

Giving someone a serious pounding doesn't take very long. I think it was over in twenty seconds. Recovering from it's another story. And this particular story looked like it would be a long one. As soon as I hit the ground, bastard number one leapt out of his truck and started raining kicks on me while bastard number two continued marking time with his stick like some kind of psychotic metronome. They took off at full throttle, spraying up gravel and dust. I stayed lying down for a moment in the light of a street lamp, letting the cloud of their hasty departure settle on my wounds.

You'll think twice about doing that next time, you fucker! These were number one's parting words. Personally I'd have liked a few more details. Who were these hired heavies? They were pretty professional when it came to brute force, but there was room for improvement on the communication side. Were they Audrey's cousins? Mr. Paul's employees? An old debt that had tracked me down? That's the danger when you have a full life, it's hard to keep track of who you're dealing with.

I wanted to roll onto my side to support myself so I could get up. I froze on the first attempt. Those fuckers had busted my ribs! My movement was extremely limited. But I couldn't stay there lying at the side of the road waiting for help. The police would roll up, probably with an arrest warrant. And if not, they'd make one up. They're allergic to young guys wandering around villages with gloves, tools, and masks. They get ideas.

I wiped the blood that was dripping over my eyelid and,

in one movement, without allowing myself to drop back to the ground, I sat up. I was made tough. I was crying, but it had nothing to do with my pain threshold. These tears were physical, maybe even mechanical. The body lubricates itself so it can get its engines running again. Sitting up, I was halfway there. I felt myself all over with my blood-smeared palms to figure out where the trickle was coming from. I shoved my fingers right into a wound at the hairline, above my right eye. That would leave a nasty scar. I had a cut on my elbow and I was also pissing blood from my broken nose. I don't know who was behind it, but he'd got himself some good subcontractors. They knew how to wallop somebody. I'd get my revenge on somebody else. The wheel turns, and I believe in karma. In the meantime, I added two anonymous assholes to my blacklist.

In three minutes I was on my feet. It took nearly as long to take the first step, but once I'd got going I hit a good cruising speed and headed back to Nicole's. I hadn't lost morale. Even the Knights Templar suffered their share of loss and injury.

7

ORGANIZATIONAL SKILLS

Breathing's enjoyable. That's something you only fully appreciate with broken ribs and a broken nose, which is quite restricting and puts things into perspective. My morning phlegm was already pretty stained from cigarettes and other substances, and now it was a masterpiece of contemporary art.

Nicole desperately tried to convince me to go to the doctor, but I reassured her that she was all the nurse I needed. Bandages would be enough to close the wounds, the busted nose would add something to my style, and anyway, you can't do anything for the ribs. *Time sorts everything out, my beautiful Nicole.* I took advantage of the situation to borrow yet more money from her and to send her out to do my shopping. While she was out looking for beer and cigarettes, I got the village dealer over to replenish my supplies of amphetamines and pot. Excellent product, considering it was local. I managed to get a bit of stock saved up too. It was a period of abundance. And of unbearable pain.

During the first few days it was difficult for me to relieve my sexual tension myself, because of my fucked-up elbow and ribs. Helped by a mixture of amphetamines, wine and beer, I revealed my difficulties to Nicole, who was drinking with me at the time. I got her to understand, in veiled terms, that she could be of great help to me in this respect. She hadn't had a young guy in several decades. I found a taker and she took me.

The body has obsessions that the heart doesn't approve of. Nicole was old and chubby, but I could make out her earlier beauty from another time. She was a gentle woman, full of little kindnesses for me. She deserved at least this much. I was performing an act of charity.

Lying on her bed, way more comfortable than my own, I made it my duty to keep my eyes closed, open my mind, and rummage through my bank of salacious pictures. Nicole was all about the little tongue licks and sighs. When she finally straddled me, I compared her niece's skinniness to the corpulence of her body. I felt myself sinking into the mattress. Curious, I opened my eyelids, but shut them again immediately. Too late. I'd seen the beast. Contrary to my usual habit, I knew that I wouldn't be able to ejaculate quickly. After stimulation comes simulation. I faked a polite orgasm and complained of rib pain. She withdrew with difficulty and apologized.

No, no, it was good. No need to apologize… There's still a bottle of red left to open, right?

Hi, Mama, do you recognize me? You're beautiful. No.

Hey, Mom, I finally found you. You hid yourself well. Not that either.

Mama, we can finally tell social services to go fuck themselves and spend some time together. Are you happy? If I was ill at ease in front of my own mirror, I could barely imagine a successful reunion in the flesh. I tried to reassure myself by telling myself it was just my face upsetting me. One eye was still swollen, my lips slightly split, and I couldn't get used to the curve, or rather the bend, of my new nose.

It's been so long, we must have so much to catch up on! No, that wouldn't do, I abandoned the rehearsal and rolled a joint. Then another one.

Once I was relaxed my ideas were clearer. Imagining this meeting would get me nowhere—I had to make it happen. Great events aren't planned, they're lived. *Come to the West, we'll do the rest,* as Alice Cooper sang. All I had to do was go to Sherbrooke, show up on Prospect Street, knock on the door, and let destiny take care of the rest. Blood ties are thicker than anything, it's well documented. I rolled a third, then stretched and tested how well my joints were recovering. I was capable of pleasuring myself. It was decided. I would leave tomorrow.

Tomorrow was yesterday. I drank too much, smoked too much, fucked Nicole again. I didn't even want to, but when it's there for the taking... And there was a precedent. And alcohol, and fatigue. I'm not looking to justify myself here. Absolutely not much at all.

Like dogs, humans stay stuck together for a certain amount of time after the act. That's what life wants. We went all the way this time. It felt as though it had popped my ribs. It was really painful. Turns out I was going to wait until Monday for the grand departure. That worked better, Monday rhymes with getaway. While I waited, I'd let fat Nicole pamper me and I'd find some funds for the trip.

Like the flower, bloom where God plants you. That's Christian. It goes for criminals too. No matter which way I turned things, I couldn't see any quick scheme for coming up with some ready cash in my state, and the first of the month was still a long way off. Monday had arrived. I made a withdrawal from Nicole's handbag.

She never got up before nine or ten. It was perfect, the intercity coach left at quarter past eight. I'd turned Nicole down after the second bottle of wine. She'd been pretty disappointed. I get it. I gulped down three pills to be sure of not falling asleep and stashed the remaining alcohol in my bag. When the first rays of sun appeared I passed go and collected nearly two hundred dollars from her purse.

I was limping toward the famous convenience store where the bus would pick me up when I noticed the blood on the road. In spite of a rainy night, my hemoglobin had stained the asphalt. It had flowed from the road right to the gravel shoulder. I took some pride in that. I'd marked the village, in a way. Then I left it without any further ceremony.

Once I was settled at the back of the bus, calculating the cash I had left after paying the fare—daylight robbery—I felt fatigue overtake me. I had to force myself to stay awake as far as Drummondville, where I would change for Sherbrooke. I was hypnotized by the kilometres of road and forest.

I wandered round the station in Drummondville. The bus nearly drove off without me. The driver opened the door and threw me a scornful look. I demanded his name before heading to my seat. I'd get revenge on him too, one of these days. I really needed to update my list and get it written down. Otherwise I might forget it. *So many bitches and bastards will know the fury of my wrath, yeah, fuck you!* That sounded good. I had a new chorus. I needed to find a record company, RFN.

The weather was grey, the road was grey, and I was green with fatigue and hunger combined. Thirty hours without sleeping. Fifteen without eating. I should have got something to munch on at the station instead of wandering around. Too late. I watched the highway exits pass by and reminded myself that everything would be better in my new life.

It was the first time I'd ever travelled so far.

Sherbrooke. My mother's town. I got a bit misty-eyed. If she'd chosen to settle here, there must have been a reason. This place had to be like her or be dear to her. I set foot in it with a certain amount of restraint. I entered my mother's city respectfully.

Once I'd relieved myself, I turned to look in the mirror. My face was still swollen. My clothes were dirty. I should have asked Nicole to take care of that before I left. I had bags under my eyes too. I needed a coffee, a hot bath, and a bed with crisp white sheets. I left the station whistling a Nickelback tune.

The good thing about bus terminals located right downtown is that you soon come across community workers. I sucked one in with my usual story of a breakup and a job loss on top of a bone disease, and in no time he was going out of his way to find me somewhere to stay. Even transport was provided. He went with me to the big homeless shelter, where I had to argue with the social worker to get a bed. I didn't have a piece of photo ID or a guarantor.

I piled on a few layers of good sentiments and a scarcely veiled suicide threat to make the employee fold. The tiny room was clean and the conditions acceptable: no drugs or alcohol, and I had to leave during the day, between 8:00 a.m. and 6:00 p.m. If I stayed for more than a week we'd have to write up an intervention plan for finding me somewhere to live. *With pleasure, man.* I headed toward the soup kitchen, then took advantage of my first night in the town of infinite possibilities to sleep the sleep of the righteous.

The little social worker from the previous day came to wake me up. I muttered and pretended to go back to sleep. He was persistent. *We even left you longer. You seemed so tired. But now you really have to get up. The centre's closed during the day.*

Getting my body up was difficult. I dragged myself to the showers, spat up my daily blood, and made the most of my morning erection for relaxation purposes. Unbelievably, the

Pomeranian on duty even came to harass me while I was in the shower. He called me by my current borrowed name. I didn't respond to it right away. The dawn mists. *Are you talking to me?*

You've been in there for more than twenty minutes, you need to hurry up. We're closing for the day. Life is hard for travellers.

I looked for a source of income as I wandered around the town. The women and the sunshine distracted me from my quest. I had to stop frequently. With the number of skirts and leggings I was seeing, I'd never manage to come up with a good plan for the day. I needed money. For self-medication and to buy flowers for my mother. You don't show up to visit someone empty-handed. You need flowers or a weapon, it's well documented. While I waited, I decided to take advantage of the air conditioning in the municipal library.

Make the most of the present. Read the signs. Master Eckhart would have encouraged me to seize the opportunity. As soon as I went into the entrance hall, the notice board jumped out at me. I never usually bother reading those little messages and the ads for shows by really bad local artists, but that day a logo caught my eye. In the jobs corner. The Eastern Townships SPCA was looking for an animal health technician. The Society for the Prevention of Cruelty to Animals. Sixteen bucks an hour. No doubt about it, it was the perfect job for me.

I had a lot of experience. But it wasn't exactly the kind of experience you can put on a resumé. Thanks to social networks and the stupidity of the average citizen, I found an identity for my CV without any trouble. The guy was originally from Mascouche, had got his college diploma two years earlier, and even listed his last employer. His moronic friends had been wishing him happy birthday a month earlier. The whole deal. Our ages matched, I added a fictional employer, and I was holding in my hands the ideal curriculum vitae for an animal health technician. To bring me luck, and because I had to put in an address, I gave my mother's. I was really excited about the idea of getting my first job. I stopped off in the toilets before I left.

The convenient thing about the municipal library, in addition to all those books to read, the internet access, and the girls wearing skirts, was that it was just a couple of steps away from a junk shop. A junk shop that bought books, at low prices but in bulk. I stuffed my bag at the library and unloaded it five buildings away. It's not just the economy that has to keep going, it's literature too.

And on top of this, just a few doors down from the junk shop was Rob N Kurt's pub. I immediately discovered that it was the ideal place to stock up on amphetamines for a good price. Other interesting substances were on offer, but my needs pushed me to the pills, whose effect is powerful and long-lasting. I smoke and drink too, like everyone does. We all need a crutch. Life is unbearable without support.

This little Bermuda Triangle in the Eastern Townships had basically saved my life. But like any good criminal or business-man, I would need to diversify.

8

RECOGNITION

My mother had short hair, which I don't usually like. I prefer it when women play up their sex with long hair, delicate features, and skirts. But I still thought she was pretty, maybe because she was my mother. She was calm, moving around her apartment with a light step, doing everything gently. Maybe she wasn't so devoted to psychiatry anymore. She watched television and ate sunflower seeds almost every evening. She often talked on the phone too.

After spying on her for three evenings, I started to recognize her expressions, her smiles. It was my mama. I was ready to bet on it and pay for a maternity test.

She'd changed, put on weight and aged, but she was still a beautiful woman. I was eager to meet her officially, and see her face fill with wonder as she recognized me. But for the time being I wanted to get my bearings and get to know her in her own space.

She lived in the basement of a triplex and covered her windows with see-through white curtains. I'd have to warn her that it wasn't safe, that she was exposing herself to thieves and perverts. The thought of protecting my mother made me proud.

That evening, I stayed crouching by the window for close to three hours, until she went to bed and turned off all the lights. I hummed her a lullaby. I couldn't remember all the words so I improvised. My mind is very quick. A seductive tranquility came over me for a moment.

I limped back to the centre feeling at peace. I whistled "Dear Mama" by Tupac Shakura. It's sad that the government had him assassinated. He was a great artist, Tupac. But he was too much of a pacifist. Like John Lennon and Malcolm Luther King. The government just can't let these pacifist artists live. It's an economics thing.

I arrived at the centre, my head full of my mother and international issues. I was stopped short by a closed door and the Pomeranian refusing to let me in. It was too late, the rules were clear and strict. I'd have to contact the emergency shelter if I needed somewhere to stay the night. I swore I'd throw myself under the next train instead, and spent a warm night in my closet.

Still no reply from the SPCA. They'd had my CV for three days already, for fuck's sake! Did they need a technician or not? While I was at the library I checked the messages in my eight other email accounts.

There were still several women from Côte d'Ivoire who were dying to marry me, I'd won hundreds of thousands of euros yet again and just needed to claim my prize, and, of course, I had several offers for penis enlargement. This last one always bothered me. I couldn't help wondering, worrying. Was it possible the advert was targeted? Had someone been informing the company about my penile proportions? I've got a big dick, no doubt about it. Not as big as Steve the Haitian or porn actors, but I'm pretty certain I've got a normal penis, so a big one. Women love big ones, it's well documented.

Several messages from dating sites too. I'd kept my accounts active. I snooped around a bit, seeing the new candidates on the market. Nothing interesting, but I put out a few feelers to the least ugly ones.

In a more personal account I came across an email from Marie-Josée. *Rite back now ITS ERGENT.* I hate people giving me orders and I despise illiterates, so the chances of my writing back were dwindling even before I took in what she was saying. It was basically just a mishmash of insults and threats. Her aunt was having trouble because I'd never paid the rent as well as having relieved her of a small amount of cash and *running off like a thief.* But for her, the worst thing was that I was a *durty fucker.* She'd come back from a clinic with confirmation that I'd given her some infections. A smile played on my lips. Poor girl. Sex is Russian roulette, honey. No mention of Aunt Nicole's genital health. I guessed from this that they hadn't confided in one another.

She must have been diagnosed with genital herpes. I've been carrying it around for several years. Apparently it never goes away, but I'm lucky because I have hardly any symptoms. I've been told that, depending on the blood group, the level of acidity in the body, and some other factors, you can be practically asymptomatic. That's the case for me. I'm one of millions of herpes sufferers on the planet. There's really no need to make a big song and dance about it. I guess the nurse didn't reassure Marie-Josée. It's supercommon and you can get creams for it.

I did one last check of all my inboxes, and bingo, the SPCA had replied. Full of hope I opened the message: double bingo, all four corners and a horizontal line! The management wanted to meet me the following Friday at 10:00 a.m. for a job interview.

My days of poverty and stealing books from the library would soon be over. This job was tailor-made for me. On their website, I'd seen that in addition to the creatures they sold and the treatment available at the main office, they also offered home services. I'd be able to scope out houses and help myself to the petty cash. Not to mention all those abandoned animals that would be readily accessible. Bring on the relaxation!

My mother was sleeping somewhere else that night. I leaned on her windowsill, alone. It was the first time that week she'd done this to me. There were no lights on in her place, nothing to protect her from burglars. I was gripped with the desire to visit her apartment, but I'm a respectful person. I stood there, dazed, for almost two hours. Wondering where she was, and above all who she was with.

Before I went back to the centre, I rifled through her mail and took the cable bill. I could dig up some information about her and the things she liked. All the way home I kept my damp hand firmly clasped around the envelope. A treasure. A piece of my mother. I'd take my time scrutinizing every inch of it.

That night I didn't sleep. I read and reread her name ceaselessly. Marie-Madeleine Fournier. I didn't have enough neurotransmitters to control all the things jostling about in my brain. I'm intelligent, but there were more hypotheses than a human could handle. I was suffering from a massive hypothesis overdose.

But my mother's name was Marie-Madeleine Fontaine. Had Marie-Josée given me the wrong address? Had my mother got married? Were there other Marie-Madeline Fs in Quebec? Was she hiding under a fake name as well? Was it possible she wasn't actually my mother?

No. If she was a stranger, I wouldn't have felt so sure she was my mother. I'd recognized her facial expressions, her smile, and the way she held the phone. I was positive. It was impossible to be mistaken about it. If it wasn't her, *was* my mother even in the

Eastern Townships, or was she maybe dead like my father? No.

I could pick my mother out of a thousand mothers. I have a maternal instinct.

I'd go and see her and we'd get everything straightened out. Yes. On Saturday. Or Monday. But no need to torture myself in the meantime. There'd been too many signs, this woman was my mother and that was that!

The mixture of adrenaline, amphetamines, nicotine, and hope was keeping me from sleeping. I needed a glass of something, or two or three bottles. I needed alcohol to relax since my hand was no longer any help. I wanted to jump out a window, but they were all nailed shut. I gathered my things together and was about to go out through the main door when a social worker shouted over to me. More Doberman than Pomeranian, this one. *If you leave, you can't come back.*

I'll come back tomorrow, that's fine.

No, if you go out in the middle of the night, you're not allowed to sleep here again for a week. And you'll have to do the whole registration process over again. We have our rules, and you can't just take off like that in the middle of the night... You can't just waltz in and out whenever you feel like it.

I leapt at his throat and bit out one of his eyes. In my head. In reality I stayed nice and calm and added the Doberman-alike and the centre to my revenge list. The job interview was the next day. I needed a shower and a place to crash. Having no other choice, I went back to my bedroom grumbling.

I needed an unbelievable amount of zinc cream the next day. I hadn't closed my eyes all night. I wasn't relaxed at all.

They were practically apologetic about giving me the job. What with my college diploma and the skills I could offer, they'd have preferred to offer me a better-paid position, more related to animal care. Something would probably open up in the coming months. And in the meantime, I'd be on the road with Reynald. Like a good sport, I assured them that this arrangement suited me for now.

They made me sign a whole pile of permission forms and waivers. Then I wrote out all the information I had on my alter ego, having found out his social insurance number by phoning Service Canada, and I gave my mother's mailing address. I explained my particular circumstances. Since I'd recently been the victim of identity theft, I couldn't receive direct deposits into my account. They'd have to pay me by cheque or send it to the address on the form.

Of course, no problem. It's a pleasure to welcome you to our team. We're all like a big family here.

And there I was, an employee of the Society for the Prevention of Cruelty to Animals. An interesting job, particularly from a sociological perspective. I could observe up close the pathetic manifestation of the egocentric happiness of anthropomorphism. I'm just reading that over again and I'm rather proud of that sentence... Translation for dunces: I just want to shine a light on the stupidity and the self-centredness of Mr. and Mrs. Everyman. Especially Mrs. Everyman, when she dresses her animal in little coats or has long conversations with it.

Every day, good people came to buy cheap animals to appease their conscience. They were saving an animal from death and lack of love. Ha! There were still a hundred left behind; just to keep the numbers manageable we killed twenty-odd a week. Every month we filled a garbage container with the most adorable little creatures.

Most importantly, they got to choose their animal. And there's the rub. Nobody takes the oldest, the mangiest, or the most aggressive ones. People want a tame animal with a bright future. Their good deed gets diluted by what they reap in personal profit.

It's actually the same problem with foster families. People are keen to take their cheque and shine their halo, but they don't want the problem kids, the disabled ones, or any other demanding little brats. People want children in need, but just enough to fill their own needs. Abandoned animals and children are advised to be cute. I'm well placed to tell you this.

That afternoon, I was driving in the truck, sitting beside the infamous Reynald, small, tough, grizzled, and cranky. Too many years spent working with critters had had an effect on him. He grunted more than he spoke and scratched his crotch vigorously, like an animal. I could tell we were going to get on. I was chomping at the bit to start killing wildlife with him.

Posted at the entrance to a shopping mall, I was getting seriously bored handing out SPCA leaflets when we received our first proper call. A Rottweiler was frightening passersby at the edge of Beckett Woods. *We have to catch him and take him in a cage to the Society for the Prevention of Cruelty to Animals.* Reynald never used the short form. He was a man who like prestige. Every chance he got, he rattled off his title, his years of experience, and his feats of gunmanship. He confirmed receipt of the call and gave me his first smile of the day. It must have been an important job. *We're going to work with the police on this one.*

Attractive rings immediately appeared around my armpits. My nice little beige shirt, fresh from the depot, was getting dirty. *Why the police? It's only a dog. Aren't we capable of handling it?*

Reynald mumbled something. I started to say it again, but he cut me off and said clearly: *It was members of the public who made the complaint, they probably contacted the police directly. From what I understand, the dog is tied up but it's barking at anyone who comes near. The police have to look for the owner. Yet another bright spark who thought a fighting dog in a residential area would be a good idea.*

Reynald was speaking from experience. The situation turned out to be exactly as he'd predicted. The big black dog was slobbering as it strained on its leash, growling and barking. It was at the end of a chain fixed to a telephone pole, so the risks were small, but a child could have gone up to it and been disfigured. I let Reynald have a little chat with the cops while I got the equipment out of the truck. Telescopic stick, tranquilizer dart gun, first aid kit, and the big cage we had to trap the hound in.

The beast guessed that we weren't there to shake a paw. As soon as we approached, it started growling and biting its chain. We went forward carefully, under the admiring gaze of the police and a few curious people who sensibly stayed at the side of the road. Cerberus flattened itself against the ground, ready to jump. It was exciting. If it hadn't been for the police presence, I could have enjoyed the moment and the adrenaline rush, but I just wanted to get out before anyone took an interest in me. The deep-rooted reflex of the skilled bandit. You never know with the pigs—even when you have nothing compromising on you, they might get curious and start trying to find out your identity.

After several gentle but useless approaches, Reynald decided the dog was aggressive enough for us to use the tranquilizer darts. He handed me the little rifle he'd just loaded. *Have you done this before, young man?*

Sure, we did this all the time in college.

He looked at me suspiciously and reminded me to stand four metres away.

I was sweating all the liquid out of my body. Finding myself with a gun in my hands so close to the police was surreal. Dream and nightmare intertwined in a mystical braid. It even crossed my mind that I might be having a shamanic experience. Here was my chance to shoot at a police officer and join the ranks of my organized-crime heroes. But I could also see the dangers of the situation. Their .38 bullets would probably have a stronger calming effect than my paralyzing darts. And there were two of them. There'd be another time.

All eyes were on me. A breathless cyclist had even stopped to take photos. A trickle of sweat ran down my crack. My shirt was soaked. I had to get this over with as quickly as possible. I crouched down, rested on my knee, and shot.

Not the head, idiot! You shot it in the head!

I couldn't have known. I decided to plead legitimate defence. *The dog moved! The exact second I pulled the trigger!* Before we'd finished arguing about it, the beast was flat out on the ground snoring.

Reynald threw himself on it and took its pulse. *I hope there won't be any after-effects. I don't know what they taught you at college but you need more practice.*

I agreed, my mind elsewhere. I absolutely had to get hold of a dart gun like this for my own personal use.

9

INTIMACY

I'd never seen my mother caress a man before. I'd never even considered the idea. Nobody should have to see that kind of thing. Most so-called normal people never see it anyway. It must be some sort of innate modesty to preserve the species. Nowadays we know it's best to avoid having fantasies about your mother. A handy mechanism to prevent too much in-breeding in the great human brotherhood.

The man was burly and bearded. I wondered if it was nice when he kissed her, or if it prickled my mother's lips. Mama would have delicate lips. Slumped on top of her on the couch, he was throwing himself into it wholeheartedly. He seemed somewhat offhand to me as he doggedly groped her breasts, practically kneading them. I desperately wanted to knock on the window and rescue my mother. Maybe she wasn't enjoying it and was just waiting for the chance to free herself. I held back and turned away.

I'd already been waiting by the window when they arrived together. The man had a fancy car with a spoiler. He must have been rich. They'd laughed and kissed on the threshold before they went into my mother's apartment. I was relieved to see her come home but annoyed that she was with someone. After a good session of foreplay and wine in a corner of the apartment I couldn't see, they settled in the living room. Right under my observation post. Just as the genitals were on the point of coming out, the providential female discussion reflex was triggered. Bravo, Mama!

I scrutinized the man carefully. It was obviously his place she'd stayed at. My mother followed the rules. One man at a time, if only for reasons of hygiene. I wondered how long they'd been going out when the idea hit me right in the face. I nearly toppled over into the cedar hedge. It was my father! Maybe.

I was hairy too, and had a serious expression beneath a big brow. And I loved women by the handful, as did he. Looking at him some more, I noticed we both had the same prominent cheekbones. Fournier. So my last name could be Fournier. Was it Louis or Marco? Which of the names that had eaten away at my childhood belonged to this handsome man who was uninhibitedly fondling my mother?

I let my mother abandon her resistance and her underwear as I crouched under the window thinking and dreaming. I dreamed so hard that it covered the noise of their lovemaking.

The pieces of the jigsaw were falling into place. My mother had come to live in the Eastern Townships to find the man of her life, whose name was Fournier, first name to be determined. She'd married him and taken his name, hence abandoning Fontaine. They had no doubt tried to contact me, but the fuckers at social services had stopped them. And now I, in my determination, had come to them.

We were going to get our family together again.

My heart was banging passionately away at the door of hope. I was short of breath and my pulse was racing. This realization was incredible but was giving me vertigo. I did a few breathing exercises and treated myself to half an amphetamine and a little joint to calm my nerves. I was doling the drugs out parsimoniously. I was poor, after all. But wealth is on the inside—on the inside of that apartment where my parents were waiting for me.

They'd left the living room. They were going to finish off in the bedroom. The curtains were opaque but I could make out candle halos in the trickle of light that bathed the window frame. I thought that was touching. Candles are romantic. I was reassured. My parents loved each other.

I wished them goodnight and headed off again whistling "Heart of Gold," a ballad by Phil Collins.

Cadavers are stiff and heavy. Dead bodies are amazing. Animal and human both. They're lumps of meat. You can't treat them like objects, but that's not so far off. Objects of heavy meat.

The first dog we picked up by the side of the road had been injured very recently and was a bit soft. That beast's weight was really striking and hard to handle, but the weight of death was even more noticeable with little animals. Raccoons and cats especially. You can grab them with just one hand, but as soon as you try to lift them up you realize how much life brings lightness.

Reynald told me frankly that he thought I was strange but that I was a good worker. The Rottweiler incident passed without consequence. I didn't object to hard work and wasn't afraid of any animal, alive or dead. That was all that mattered to him. I handled the dead and the injured ones with confidence, a rare quality. He liked the firmness with which I mastered the agitated animals. If I carried on like this he'd be recommending that they hire me at the end of my probation period.

I was flattered. Most of all it confirmed for me that I didn't need a diploma. My entire childhood, people had tried to make me believe that my brain was deficient. And now I was working as a professional with a ton of responsibilities. Put that in your pipe and shove it up your ass, my dear counsellors.

I do things intuitively, I'm a natural, as they say. Diplomas are only good for boosting talentless people's self-esteem. It's taxpayer-funded brainwashing, that's all. Einstein didn't do a PhD in relativity. No great author studied literature. Even the saints had no theological education. In life, you've either got it or you haven't. And I've got it.

Despite my talent, I didn't intend to work for very long. However, Reynald almost made me want to. I liked people noticing my good points, and after his third coffee he was decent company.

I managed to survive by shoplifting alcohol from the supermarket and pawning trinkets I'd stolen from nearby stores, as well as the occasional complete collection from the library. The idea of settling down to a stable job at the SPCA crossed my mind the same way you cross the street—fairly quickly. I remembered where I'd come from, my principles and my values. I didn't want to be anyone's peon just to enrich the system. I don't believe in work, it's a form of modern slavery. I've read Richard Marx. He's an author who's really down on capitalism.

And I knew that one day I'd re-enter the ranks of organized crime. For now, though, it was fun roaming in the truck with Reynald, waiting for my first paycheque and driving dead animals around.

We also had to deal with live animals. Even if we ended up killing the majority of the ones we brought in. There are so many abandoned animals. And no laws to condemn the irresponsible people who throw them out when they move house. It shows how stupid our legal system is. We have this whole setup to punish thieves who are just trying to survive, but do nothing about the bastards who abandon living creatures by the side of the road.

People don't mean to be bad, young man.

Exactly! That's worse! It's better if you know something's bad when you do it. There's nothing worse than the spinelessness of all those people who can't even be bothered to look at themselves in the mirror.

Well, you've certainly got some resentment stored up, haven't you. Things aren't always black and white, you know. You'll see what I mean in a few minutes.

I was still arguing. Until we stopped in front of a building with a dozen apartments in the Centre-Sud, a poor neighbourhood. Reynald sniggered, then held out a pot of echinacea cream to me. *Stick a bit of that under your nose, young man. It doesn't exactly reek of happiness around here.* I refused, insisting that I had strong nerves and that I never accepted cream from a man. He smiled at me and said again that I was weird.

Mrs. Picard is slightly crazy. She's not a bad person but she has to take medication and she often forgets. After a few days she starts collecting cats. She gathers all the strays in the neighbourhood and even catches ones with name tags.

I nodded to show him I was interested.

Pleased with the effect he was having, Reynald carried on. *It's probably going to take us all morning. She's already gone away for a little psychiatric holiday. We have to get all the cats out, make sure there aren't any hidden, shut them in cages, and bring them all back to headquarters.*

I approved with another nod of the head and congratulated myself on having taken two pills before I went to work. It looked like we had an unpleasant program ahead.

Ammonia hit the back of my throat when the caretaker opened her door for us. I took a step back and crashed into the banister. Reynald took his cream out of his pocket again, but I refused it once more. I'm a proud man. The janitor covered his nose, wished us good luck, and then closed the door behind him. Cat piss and shit covered almost the entire living room carpet and all the kitchen tiles. The bedroom door was closed. Some scrawny cats approached us, meowing fit to break your heart, while others hid under the furniture. We put the four cages down.

Last time we found thirteen. The smell wasn't as strong as this and that was right in the middle of a heat wave. I reckon we're going to break that record today. Reynald rubbed his hands together, already full of a sense of duty that eluded me.

Wearing gloves up to our elbows, we filled the first cages and made one trip and then another. We had our dozen, we'd have to unload the truck and come back again.

Poor woman, Reynald murmured. *Poor crazy lady,* I thought. Madness is a bit like homosexuality, you deny it or you let it move right in. Nobody has to be something they don't want to be. *Everything is a matter of will,* as Socrates—a philosopher— might have said.

As we arrived for the third trip, I told Reynald I'd deal with the bedroom so that he could finish inspecting the living room and the kitchen. With the door and windows closed, the smell was even riper. I covered my mouth and nose but it didn't help. The stench got in everywhere, even into the pores of my skin. I wanted to throw up and then give in and accept Reynald's cream, but I managed to overcome these weaknesses. Socrates would have been proud.

I found the first two dead cats. A ginger, curled up at the bottom of the bed, and then a pale grey one huddled by a chest of drawers. I rummaged eagerly through the drawers, but they contained nothing of interest. I moved right on to the bedside tables. I pocketed a few jewels from a bygone era. Picard wasn't just crazy, she was also old. I'd have to sell her scrap metal by weight. I was heading toward the dresser when I heard meow-ing coming from under the bed. I bent over and saw two other scrawny felines. I hurried to check out the dresser, but no luck. Coming back from the living room, where I'd picked up two bags and two cages, I noticed that one of the cats had climbed onto the unmade bed.

I approached softly, holding my arms out toward it. He must have been related to the dead ginger. He was calm, but as soon as I grabbed him he started to struggle, scratching and arching his back. My stiff gloves meant I couldn't get a good grip. He escaped and climbed up my arm to my shoulder. Before I could get hold of him, he'd scratched my neck. A second later, I'd broken his.

I went back to the living room with one cage and two bags. *Turns out there were three dead ones. I'm going to take another bag.*

Reynald, crouching in front of the couch knee-deep in piss, agreed.

Those old jewels turned out to be valuable. Selling them meant I could leave the shelter and rent a room, six blocks from my mother's place. I was becoming responsible, and even re-establishing some financial stability. After buying thirty amphetamines for the week, three bags of Indian cigarettes, and a bottle of Jack, there was a little bit left over for food. I was practically well off. The injuries on my face were getting better. The fateful day of the reunion was approaching. Just thinking about it made my hands sweaty and my heart start galloping. I had to stroke myself to calm down.

I allowed myself two more weeks. I'd have time to cash my first paycheque and buy a real bunch of exotic flowers. I believe in astrology and omens. I'd go and meet her on her actual birthday. She'd be even more touched and the encounter would be even more significant for the two of us. Until then, I'd keep up my daily visits so I could get to know her.

My new bedroom was in the basement, as usual. Damp and dark, as usual. But it was my own room. I paid for it and lived in it. Most importantly, access was independent of the house and I was alone there for now. Since the other room to rent was vacant, I had, in effect, two bedrooms, a kitchenette, and a little living room for my sole use. A real pasha master of my own kingdom. I settled in comfortably. I decided it was time to get seriously solvent with a proper burglary.

Mama was alone. She was chatting on the phone and watching an episode of *CSI: Miami*. I really wanted to taste her spaghetti. She'd browned it in the oven and had to blow on each mouthful, it was so hot. I imagined us sitting facing each other during our first meals. We had so much to tell each other. But I wouldn't tell her everything, not right away. After a few weeks I'd move next to her so we could watch television as a family. Mama would have to explain the plots to me since I'm not a big watcher of series. I would learn.

She seemed rather sad. I hoped the bearded man, who was probably my father, hadn't cheated on her with another woman. I was comforted by the thought that it was probably an incident at work or some other inconsequential thing.

I'd been crouching there for nearly three hours. I like TV evenings, but when there's no sound, you can only see a corner of the screen and you're all folded up, it gets tiring. I was stiff, and had pins and needles in my legs, so I hopped about for a couple of minutes to bring myself back to life, then set off to burgle her neighbour.

During the period I'd been camping out under Mama's window, I'd had time to stake out the surroundings. On the other side of the cedar hedge where I hid to get to know my mother stood another triplex, also beige and brown. Every weekday evening at nine forty-five, the lights on the second floor went off and a young woman in her early thirties tore down the stairs and raced off, tires squealing. Late for work. She must have had a night shift in a factory. Or she worked for an escort agency. That idea got me excited.

As accurate as a Belgian clock, she left her apartment at the appointed time. I left my mother to her television, murmuring a few kindly words in her direction, hoping some god would protect her. I'm very Christian.

I climbed the stairs like a real ninja, barely making the treads creak, then hunched over by the door and tried to manipulate the lock. It's not as easy as it looks in the movies. As a matter of fact, this particular lock was impossible to pick. I wasn't going to make a fuss about it. I broke the window by giving it a good whack with a screwdriver and waited for a reaction from the neighbours. Nothing, as usual. Individualism and cocooning—blessings to the modern burglar.

After a short wait, I plunged my arm inside, reached the lock, and invited myself into the warmth. It was a pleasant apartment, nice and tidy. I like clean people. There were cookies on the stove in a glass dish. Chocolate ones. Delicious. I was about to leave the kitchen to explore the other rooms when I noticed that the window above the sink looked straight into my mother's living room. I could even see her feet, the carpet, a bit of the low table, and the television. I was feeling all the feels. I hadn't seen my mother's bare feet since I was a kid.

There was a small television on the counter. I soon found the channel Mama was watching. I turned up the volume and followed the plot from one screen to the other. It was a family activity. The taste of blood filled my mouth. I realized I'd been gnawing my nails so much I'd drawn blood, so happy was I to be sharing this moment with my biological mother.

After the ad break the main character realized he'd been duped by the assassin. The latter had spread the DNA of an as-yet-unfound victim at the scene of a more recent murder. The police had been going round in circles for weeks. *Good work, ha!* But then the cocky investigator collared him. *Too bad.* Mom turned it off as the credits started and went to bed. I took another cookie, and went off to the bedroom nibbling.

It was too clean. No worn undergarments. I pocketed a pair of lacy ones and some jewellery. I found a big scrapbook. It was pretty, very colourful with sparkles and all that stuff. Full of family photos. The woman who lived here was sensual, her emaciated face making her plump lips stand out. Near the end there were photos of a wedding or a dance. Her clinging purple dress caught my attention.

In the living room, I found nothing but a few art films. I was disappointed. I took them anyway, culture's important. Auteur films are deathly dull but useful for your vocabulary. Like the great classics. I also took a rather nice edition of *The Human Comedy*. Just the first two volumes—I was hardly going to read the whole thing.

Back then I didn't know there was a long sentence in my future. When I'm inside I'm going to get through all of Balzac, and Harry Potter too.

I didn't need to stay any longer in the apartment. I just hoped the jewellery would be worth something. I took one last cookie for the road.

10

INVOLVEMENT

Reynald was in a really good mood that morning. He was telling me all about how proud he was to have been nominated to head up Dr. Héroux's team of volunteers. He told me the doctor was a noted sovereigntist, likely to become a minister. This idea really excited him, and his usual mumblings gave way to lyrical flights on building the future of the country. I agreed, and even outdid him a bit to get myself into his good books.

Quebec must be liberated as soon as possible.

Yes, young man, that should have been done a long time ago.

You're right, Reynald! Let's distance ourselves from that Canadian mistake and take up the struggle once more. We shall overcome!

Reynald was enjoying himself so much he was wriggling in his seat. I actually thought he was pretty ridiculous, like all sovereigntists. A bit pathetic, and completely unrealistic too. We have no reason to leave Canada. Canada's a great country. And we're just a little pack of losers speaking French at the edge of the ocean. If it weren't for the Anglos making the economy work and speaking the language of business, we'd have been invaded a long time ago. We don't even have an army. A country without an army is like a woman without breasts, it just attracts problems. It's well documented.

Reynald filled me in on the placard war and the importance of mobilizing voters by phone. *You're going to vote, right?*

Of course. I would never line up to mark an X that would never change anything. I quoted Coluche to get a reaction from him. *If democracy could change the world, the secret service would have crushed it a long time ago.* He argued that Coluche never said that. Rather than show him how stupid he was, I reminded him that despite his nice little country project, his doctor would be far more useful in a hospital. He disagreed completely, saying it was society that was sick. For once we were in accord. All we lacked was agreement about the treatment. He opted for idealism while I preferred bloodletting.

Reynald had started in on a soliloquy about another party's corruption when we received our first call. He immediately scowled. *Speaking of sick, we have to go to the puppy mill in Durham.*

You know it?

It's the fourth time we've been to that village. It's too lucrative for them to shut up shop. They just move their stock.

I said, *Maybe it's their competitors taking over. Happens all the time in drug dealing. Could be the same thing with dog trafficking.*

Reynald grunted. *Bernese mountain dogs, you mark my words. I'm sure it's the same gang.*

We drove along in silence. Lost in our thoughts about trafficking and politics. We were almost there when Reynald asked me if I had a girlfriend. *No, I don't want one.*

He smiled at me. *Neither do I, you know.* No, I didn't know, and I didn't know how to reply. I guessed he'd been through a nasty breakup.

The barn was at the end of a bumpy country road. Lane 11. We could see a big white house with a huge building right next to it. Clearly you could get rich no matter what you trafficked.

I had to hurry up and find my own niche. I felt the business dragon stirring in my bowels. As we got closer, I saw the police cars. *The police again?*

Yes, of course. This kind of business is a serious crime, young man. Seems like you have some kind of problem with the police?

I tried to smile, betrayed by my sweat glands. *No, no, I have no problem with them. And they have no problem with me either.* There might not have been any complaints, after all. But I doubted it. What with the stealing from Nicole, the permanent borrowings from the library, the burglaries, and everything else that had been going on, I must have left some kind of trace.

Reynald parked beside them, raising up a little cloud of dust that annoyed the cops. Bravo, Reynald! A policewoman came straight over to us. Her colleague was interviewing a couple in their sixties in front of the barn. After brief introductions, she began explaining to us the seriousness of the situation. We'd have to call for reinforcements from another town. They'd counted fifteen or so corpses, but more importantly there were almost thirty puppies in terrible condition. Reynald muttered, swore a bit, and decided we could handle the situation ourselves. We wouldn't call in another Society for the Prevention of Cruelty to Animals. Our team was enough. I learned that there was a bank of names of families willing to take in and care for injured animals. That disgusted me. Seriously, foster families for animals when there's a shortage of them for humans? Worse still, the ones they park children in are poor or dangerous. I'd have been better off being born as a Bernese mountain dog.

Reynald had called it correctly, at least in part. The majority were mountain dogs, but there were also some Labradors. The mountain-dog corpses were easier to handle, you could grab hold of their fur. I filled the bags while Reynald gave first aid to the worst off. Although they're less noble, dead dogs stink less than dead cats. We've domesticated them right down to the smell of their corpses. Personally I identify more with cats. Even after nine thousand years of domestication they're still independent and they've kept their predatory instincts. Dogs are totally stupid. Tongues always hanging out, only good for fetching a ball or a stick. No—me, I'm a wildcat.

I was philosophizing as I gathered up the inert fly- and larva-ridden lumps when the cameras showed up. Newsrooms train tactical teams, who knew! Without us noticing, two different teams had invaded the barn and were filming all over with the policewoman trailing after them.

They're filming us, Reynald, they're filming us! I walked sideways to avoid the camera lens. I didn't need anyone seeing me. I dragged a corpse into a corner so I could turn my back to them and look busy.

Calm down, young man, it's perfect. We have to tug on people's heartstrings, that's what brings in donations. And it also reminds those sons of bitches who run these puppy mills that we always find them in the end. Do you want to give an interview?

I didn't get that he was joking and I almost shouted, *No!*

He laughed. *You're weird, young man, very weird…*

On our first trip back, we started off talking about the road conditions and then detoured toward car breakdowns. He told me for the first time about his passion for old cars, which he fixed up and sold. He sure liked obsolescence. Sovereignty and antique cars! He was lacking in polish, old Reynald. Sticking with my usual custom, I pretended to find him extremely interesting and asked him several questions without listening to the answers. He let slip that he'd made too many acquisitions recently. He needed to sell a couple of vehicles quickly.

Would you be interested?

In buying a collector's car from you?

They aren't all collector's cars, you know.

Actually, I might be interested. My last car died just before I came to work with you. But I've still got a ton of payments to make, and I also want to invest in a big project pretty soon. Do you think I could pay you in instalments?

No problem. Anyway, I know where to find you. Ha ha!

You won't be able to find me for long, my dear fellow. This was a pure gift from heaven. Get a car upfront and pay it off a hundred bucks every paycheque. And I was only planning on sticking around for one or two paycheques max. Pretty good price for a hot rod.

A '92 Dynasty Chrysler, brown and beige. A collector's car, after all. You'd swear it was some Bronx gangsta rapper's car—no, make that Brooklyn! To the uncultured, it was just a big brown car. I couldn't blame the ignoramuses who knew nothing about hip-hop culture, it was only the most accomplished artistic movement of the last century, maybe even of the whole history of humanity. But I knew that a big brown-and-beige car with chrome rims was classy.

I was proud. My first car. I really was becoming a man, a real one. Acquiring one's first vehicle is a rite for men. Like menstruation for women, it emphasizes the fact that you've become an adult, and it's gratifying. You want people to know about it. I strutted my stuff, cruising around in my car, the radio at full volume. I turned it down when the song was less appropriate. Björk isn't exactly gangsta enough. I drove slowly so people would really notice me. I should disclose here that I'd never had driving lessons or even driven very much before. I learned on the job, as usual.

One morning of glorious sun and short skirts, I was driving around the high schools looking for a nymphette to impress. I was also doing a bit of burglary reconnaissance. I took note of the houses whose yards backed onto woods. I located the more isolated residences. I even spotted a few businesses I could hold up. I still hadn't done that yet. It seemed like the logical next step. Stop fucking around with jewels and game consoles that had to be sold off and take the money directly. After all, my plan wouldn't be wrecked by baton-wielding bastards every time. I was thinking about this as I sat wedged in my padded bench, getting my back massaged by little wooden balls. I was the king of the town. It woke up my appetite.

It's amazing being able to run errands without ever getting out of your car. That's what the American Dream is all about. That's what Kennedy was dreaming about before he got his head blown off. The freedom to eat whatever you want wherever you want. I devoured my fries straight from the bag, watching the comings and goings in the parking lot. I'd left the engine running. You should always be ready to gun it. Plus it showed I had no money worries. That often impresses women.

I noticed one coming out of the gas station. I was driving over to her when two teenagers approached her. I parked quickly, abandoned my meal, and leapt out of the car.

Are these youths bothering you, miss? She was way less beautiful close up, but I'd make do. She was an old lady, forty at least. I emphasized the *miss*, knowing I'd get points for making her feel young. Women will do anything to knock off a few years.

No, no, it's fine. But I can't help them. Goodbye.

Wait, miss, I'll come with you! I gave the youths the eye and walked by the woman's side as far as her car. *I noticed you from a long way off, you know, you shine like the sun.*

Right, well…thanks, have a nice day. And two seconds later she had taken refuge in her car. Frigid old cow. I turned back to the youths out of curiosity but also for a challenge. The day was lacking in spice and the amphetamines were vastly increasing my sense of initiative.

Hey, guys, what did you want from that chick? The taller of the two showed me a ten-dollar bill and lisped that they wanted a pack of Peter Zacksons, and that I'd be really cool if I bought one for them. I agreed, enjoying the air conditioning while I queued. In front of me, two buff guys in work clothes were discussing municipal politics. I thought of poor Reynald and his dream of a country. At the cash, I chose Craven "A," my favourite brand, and two lottery tickets.

I walked past the kids without looking at them. They stood up immediately and called out. *Hey! Hey…you got our smokes?*

Yes, hang on, I'm just going to get something from my car. They stuck to my heels. I got in my car and signalled to them to wait a minute. They stayed right there, puzzled. I started the engine and drove out of the parking lot. In the rear-view mirror I could see them waving their arms frantically in alarm.

I lit myself a cigarette, swallowed two cold fries, and savoured the American Dream. It tasted good.

Reynald was cranky. It was going to be a long day. We had to go back to the puppy mill in Durham. The police had managed to get all the cages permanently confiscated. Of course, we were the ones who got to pick them up since we'd keep all the equipment that could be reused. Reynald explained that it was part of a program aimed at compensating victims for the losses they suffered at the hands of criminals. His disparaging tone toward the latter hurt me.

People have a lot of prejudices about criminals. It's all nonsense, everyone envies us our thrilling lives. One out of every two films and books is about us. An entire industry thrives because of television shows about us. So it's hypocritical to judge us. Anyway, criminals are probably the biggest upholders of the law. It's true. The majority of criminals, maybe even all of them, have themselves been victims of injustice or sexual abuse. They redistribute. They take back their share. You have to at least recognize that.

Reynald cut my lecture short, assuring me that society would collapse if we started respecting criminals. We didn't even have time to spit on them that day. The work was hard, it was hot in the barn. By silent agreement we adopted the same rhythm. Slow. Very slow. We stretched out our breaks and took nearly two hours to eat dinner in a nearby village. We took it so slow that we hadn't finished by the end of the day. There were still cages bolted to the walls and ground, as well as bags of stale dog food to take away. We wouldn't have time for any more trips. Reynald cursed when he said it was time to stop. I stole a metal saw as we left. Just to keep my hand in.

The following day, instead of going back to the puppy mill, I took a leave day to spy on my mother. It was time to investigate her professional life. She had to be a child-care worker or nurse or cashier. Something noble. The unknown is exciting. I had everything to discover, so I was very excited.

I'd overdone it again the night before and had only got two hours' sleep. I was used to four. My congested bronchial tubes spat out copious amounts of mucus and blood. Even with the tap at full pressure, it stayed stuck to the porcelain of the sink. I took advantage of that to call in to work, my voice as hoarse as anything.. I left a long message on the answering machine. I emphasized that they should say hi to Reynald and make sure he knew I was sorry. I hurried to get some breakfast, a slice of white bread with butter, and two amphetamines with chocolate milk. Milk is good for you, they say.

I arrived just in time, it was a sign. I watched her leave the triplex and get into her car, a white Yaris, very feminine. As soon as she left the driveway I followed her. I kept a short distance between us, so as not to lose her but without being spotted. At six o'clock there was practically nobody on the roads, but I still pulled it off like a pro. It was my first time tailing someone. We drove for ten minutes or so, then stopped in front of a breakfast-and-lunch restaurant. A pun on the word *egg* appeared in the place's name. Nice.

I was afraid she'd noticed me, since there were only four cars including both of ours. She glanced in my direction before running toward the restaurant. She must have been late. I certainly recognized myself in that. Always daydreaming and thinking about the world, never noticing the time passing. Oh, Mama, we're going to get on so well.

I procrastinated in the parking lot for a few long minutes. What should I do? I wanted to see her up close, even talk to her if I could. I was also afraid she'd recognize me, that our reunion would end up taking place between two omelettes and a fat-free yogourt. My cleverness was still playing tricks on me, I was drowning in a flood of scenarios and it was paralyzing me. I decided to go and think about it some more, afraid she'd spot me from inside and wonder why I was waiting to approach her. It wasn't the right moment to reveal myself.

Two streets over, in the shade of a big oak, I stared at my reflection. I needed to get into the habit of sleeping. The bags under my eyes were deep and purple. My lips had become chapped and red from biting them and grinding my teeth. I was obsessed with scratching my zits. This tic had left me with some nasty wounds and crevices in my skin. Although my drug habit wasn't a cause for concern, it was still affecting my appearance. Add to that the wonky angle of my broken nose, and the whole ensemble might be a bit off-putting.

These aesthetic considerations troubled me. Sadness mingled with excitement about meeting my mother. Tiredness must have played a part too, because I started trembling. I even had spasms in one calf. I needed to relax, relax, relax. I was repeating this order to myself, compulsively, when fate intervened. I hadn't noticed the bus stop a few metres away from me. A mother and her daughter came up to it.

The little girl must have been around ten or twelve. I didn't really take much notice of her, too young. I do have values and principles. So I focused on the mother. She started glancing in my direction without suspecting what I was doing. I still have all that experience stored behind my zipper. The mother was pretty fleshy, kind of plump. I could make out the large areolas around her nipples. I pictured myself on top of her, using her weight to rock myself in and out of her body.

I moaned and straightened up. It was time for brunch.

11

ALTRUISM

I have endless admiration for waitresses. Especially the old ones. Their work is physical, almost athletic. In spite of varicose veins, worn-out knees, and cramps, they spend hours standing up, exerting themselves to serve strangers. I'll say it again, it's admirable. It's a vocation more than a career. It must take guts to sacrifice their health in service to others. I was proud of my mother.

I watched her flitting from table to table, her hands full of hot plates. Mama was even able to smile while she worked. That's what we're like, that strength of character. I stayed near the gilded sign telling me to wait for someone to show me to a table. Finally it was my turn. I was waiting for my mother, but Monique, with her silly little fixed grin, turned up. I hated her on sight. *Follow me.*

I didn't have a choice. It would have aroused suspicion if I'd asked for a different waitress or demanded to be seated in a different section. I followed Monique the mountain and took my place regretfully. I consoled myself by reading the egg puns in the menu. The restaurant's owners had really given it their all.

I wasn't there to eat but I had to make an effort. Amphetamines wake up your senses, sharpen your libido, and bring you to new levels of consciousness, but they suppress your appetite. You can't have everything. I was muscular but skinny. One meal a day was enough for me. And I'd already eaten some bread. I knew that any food would just roll around in my mouth.

Hesitation is man's downfall. I'm quoting myself, but I think it's along the same lines as the ideas of Plato and Gilgamesh. In practice, it put serious pressure on my uncertainty. I didn't want anything, even though everything looked delicious. Monique came back for the fourth time. I was on my third coffee, two sugars and a cream. Time was running out.

Yes, yes, I know what I'm going to have. Wait a second, I won't be long. Just one more second, I know it. Okay, I'm deciding now. There. I chose the worker's special. That was fitting—I was a worker. Monique headed to the kitchen, leaving me gazing at the enormous calves that had supported her considerable bulk for decades.

My mother was more svelte. Her stomach pooched a little but her arms were still slim. For a woman who's had children, that's good going. Her evening snacks and her passion for TV series could have made her put on some chub. She had short hair, turned up at the neck, brown with blond streaks. Very classy. She was the best waitress in the restaurant, without a doubt. She walked more quickly, took orders as soon as customers closed their menus, and never let her smile falter. My mother was beautiful.

Monique deposited the steaming heap of protein on the table. Beans with pork, potatoes, cretons, scrambled eggs, sausages. What kind of sausages? Who knows! All animals were made to be eaten, it's in the Bible and it's well documented. We're too hypocritical to eat our cats and dogs, but we *could* eat them, just like the other animals. We should feed the poor with all the pets that get murdered at the SPCA. It would close the loop since it's their own four-legged friends they've abandoned between houses. But when push comes to shove we don't have the balls to follow through on our ideas.

Now I had to dig into my worker's platter. I struggled to chew and swallow. Even the decorative fruits stuck to my palate. My thoughts about nutrition weren't helping me clear my plate. Monique came over every five minutes to make sure everything was fine. I was sipping my sixth coffee. My sense that Mama was watching me was confirmed when I caught her deep in discussion with Monique near the hostess desk. The two of them turned toward me at the same time. I straightened up and tried to smile despite my tense jaw. Could she have recognized me? She must have been asking Monique if I'd told her my name. It was possible. Everything's possible, it says so in *The Secret*. I've seen the film. Three times.

I swallowed two mouthfuls of scrambled eggs. I was following my mother's comings and goings between the kitchens and the restaurant. I figured out the algorithm and stood up at just the right moment to intercept her on her way back. *Excuse me, ma'am?* She'd think I was polite.

Yes?

Could you please tell me in which direction I should proceed in order to find the washroom? I'd prepared my question well, I didn't stumble on a single word.

Just ahead on the right. She left immediately. Those plates she was carrying were heavy.

Thank you, ma'am! With these words intended to halt her mid-stride, I almost staggered to the washroom. I locked myself in. Seated on the throne, I tried to get my breath back. Tiredness and stress were catching up with me. I felt a stab of pain in my heart and I thought I was about to faint. But I was happy. The ice was broken. It really was her! My mama! I'd recognized myself in her brown eyes.

I didn't want to hang out in the restaurant forever. My mission was accomplished and I'd been there for two hours already. Rather than returning to my table, I headed straight to the cash. Monique met me there and handed me the bill, which was around ten dollars. I handed her a twenty and gave her a wink. *It's all for you.* As I expected, she was surprised and thanked me profusely. She would no doubt talk to my mother about it. Mama would be proud of my generosity.

I headed off, exhausted and satisfied with my day. I was dreaming of nothing more than a mattress and, above all, a shower. The radio turned right up, the windows open, I went back home duetting with Roxette: *life is life, lalalalalala, life is life!*

I woke up after 9:00 p.m., in pain. I felt as if I'd run a marathon carrying Monique on my shoulders. Stress and tiredness had wrung out my body. I stayed lying down and lit my wake-up cigarette. I looked back on all the images of my mother at work. I wondered what kind of good impression I'd made on her. I predicted that once our relationship had finally been re-established I'd always sit at the same table in the restaurant in memory of our first encounter. For once, I was hungry.

I whistled as I got dressed, I rolled a joint for the road and headed out to the grocery store on foot. A little exercise for my afflicted limbs. I decided to buy meat macaroni, two litres of chocolate milk, and a little pecan tart for dessert. Quite a feast. The cashier told me I was looking good. He was probably gay, but I liked it anyway.

I didn't let myself get flustered by the landlady wanting to be paid for the week. I assured her she'd have the money for this week and next as soon as I got my paycheque. I raised my voice. Playing the prole suited me.

Sure, and when are you going to get this famous paycheque?

Tomorrow. *Next week.*

When next week?

Thursday. *Friday. I'll have it all by next Friday.*

This is the last time I'm giving you credit, understand?

You can stick your rent money up your ass. *Yes, thank you so much!*

I devoured my breakfast, engrossed in a TV report on the First World War, and then I went back to bed, pressed up against the wall, my pillow in my arms. I hadn't slept so well for years, if not for centuries.

I was holding the first paycheque of my life, maybe the last one. I was ridiculously proud. The cheque wasn't even in my real name, but not only that—the amount for one week of work barely came to what I could make from one or two burglaries. And I had to give part of it to Reynald for the car. He wasted no time asking for it.

We can stop by the credit union, it's on our way. He did his business at credit unions too, the old patriot. Once upon a time, they had humanist leanings, but that had all changed a long time ago. Now they were just as rapacious and corrupt as the banks. It's well documented.

No, I only deal with banks.

We'll stop at your bank then, even if it's a bit of a detour. I'm sort of tight for cash right now, I need you to pay me today. As we agreed. He articulated clearly, emphasizing the significance of his words. Money is always important. It's the sinews of war, peace, love, life, and so on. Even for idealists. Maybe especially for them.

Yes, sure, no problem. But let's go to Money Mart instead, I've been having some trouble with the bank since my identity got stolen. I couldn't see any other way of cashing the cheque. Otherwise I'd have to make the whole cheque over to him and be a total sucker.

Reynald headed for downtown and told me his party's

strategy for getting the youth vote out. That man was bipolar. As soon as he started talking about politics or cars, he lit up and became chatty, but on every other topic of conversation he scowled and muttered. I affirmed the rightness of his idea to mobilize young militants in the Cegeps. I doubted the existence of any really political students, but it was fun to feed his delusion. *Young people are the future of the world!* I brandished my fist to emphasize my words.

Nonsense. The future is the coming hour, Grandpa. At the rate we're polluting, young people are stuck with the future we're going to leave them. And your country project won't change anything. We're way past that. The world is in the hands of multinationals. Governments can't do anything, quite the opposite. Only eco-terrorists can still give people hope. But they're getting rarer.

What are you thinking about, young man?

I could assassinate a bestselling author. That would be an efficient way of saving a forest or two. But no, I'm just as egocentric as the next guy. Everyone out for themselves. When I kill, it'll be personal. I'm no better than anyone else. *You don't want to know.*

What?

You don't want to know what I'm thinking about. I challenged Reynald with a look.

Yes, I do. I'm a curious man. Tell me what you're thinking, young man.

We're going to take up arms, get organized, kidnap some big names, and make a country, at last! We'll make it by force! They won't steal any more votes from us, no more rigged referendums! You up for it, Reynald? The coward gave a fake smile. I held his gaze and let him waver.

No, no, it doesn't work like that. You have to convince the people, we have to build the country together. Poor dreamer, we don't do anything together. It's one person against another, at every single level.

I know, I know, I was kidding. I laughed to reassure him. *With a great project like yours, no need to impose our country by force…* You could have cut the unease with a knife.

The Money Mart cashier quibbled a bit. My cheque was signed, but the only ID I had was my phony diploma and an old fake credit card. She needed a document with a photo. I reassured her with my most charming smiles, offering to do a private photo session. She made a copy of my diploma and contacted the employer, *It's standard procedure.*

Proceed away, darling. I took my money, vastly reduced thanks to her kind attentions, and went back to Reynald. I grudgingly handed over a hundred dollars. One hundred dollars is a lot of money. Twenty-five amphetamines or three two-fours or twelve packs of cigarettes or ten lap dances. It broke my heart.

He didn't even say thank you, the ungrateful bastard. We drove toward Stoke in silence. Almost. He was listening to country. Near enough.

It's no accident that money's made of paper, it burns your fingers more effectively. I'd never been able to save it, not even for a few hours. It was the first time in my life I'd had in my pocket so much cash—a few hundred dollars—that I'd earned, without being able to spend it. The day seemed to go on forever. We went around a few neighbourhoods handing out leaflets about the importance of animal ID tags. I just had half an amphetamine left in my body, taken at dawn. Nothing in my pocket. At the beginning of the afternoon I had to overcome the temptation to ditch Reynald where we were and walk back into the city.

Money is the mother of all vices, that's an ancient proverb. Those hypocrites who claim that it's not the most important thing for them just have enough of it to pretend otherwise. The working poor are fatalists. No matter the currency, no matter their location on the planet, people sell themselves, kill themselves, prostitute themselves, and agree to give up their bodies, their strength, and their health for money. I may not be any better than them, but I'm more aware and don't let myself drown in the general hypocrisy. Time, friends, and lovers move on, money stays. I had pockets full of it and I wanted to enjoy it.

On every trip back to the truck, I felt Reynald watching me out of the corner of his eye. I stayed focused and quiet. *I get the sense you're feeling a bit nervous today.*

You sense wrong, everything's fine. I didn't want to get into a conversation. One part of me was mad at him for having crippled my finances. And I'd had it up to here with working. I wanted to go back into the city and enjoy the fruits of my labour.

Say what you like, I did a psychology diploma before I retrained. I've had the right education, I'm sure there's something bothering you. Your whole body says so. I can see it in your posture too. It's called non-verbal language.

I pulled myself together and reassured him. *I've got some family problems, no big deal. I'm far away from them. It worries me, that's all.*

His face lit up with satisfaction. He was convinced he was a great psychologist, old Reynald. What a jerk. He could stick his studying where the sun don't shine.

If you need to talk, I'm here. He put his hand on my shoulder.

I drove a knife into his throat and twisted it in the wound. In my head. *Thanks, that's kind of you.*

We were getting to know each other. On the way back Reynald beamed irritatingly. He was relishing the way he'd supported me. We all cut our altruistic teeth on the next dog's neck. So he was a lover of Quebec, cars, and bogus interventions. As for me, I wanted to gobble down some amphetamines, play the slots, and get a stripper to dance.

Money burns hope as well as fingers. Two hours after arriving at the bar, I had a mere thirty bucks left in my pocket. I'd had the bright idea of stocking up on pills for the week, and the one-armed bandit had snatched all the rest of my dollars. I was hesitant to shovel in my last bit of cash. I regretted playing so big, so fast, but I had to see it through. My experience with machines couldn't let me down. It was going to pay out. Several times I'd been one fruit away from jackpot. It would be the wrong time to give up.

Debby came over and rested her prominent mammaries on the machine. What an imbecile! That's bad luck. In my head I poured out a flood of insults toward her, but I didn't even look up, hoping she'd get the message and go away. No way that was happening; she'd seen I was loaded. And I was one of very few customers in the place. Strip clubs in that part of town aren't very busy on weekday afternoons.

If you win loads of cash, will you get me to dance for you, babe?

Like you've never danced before! I thought this offer would send her off to some other sucker, but she carried on making her prosthetics prance about in front of the screen.

I'm gonna take care of your wad, you just watch. The idiot was really laying it on thick. I'd lost the rhythm and the thread of the game. I'd never find where I'd got to in the algorithm so the machine would spit my cash out. I breathed so I wouldn't explode. I had just one desire: to grab Debby by her blond mane and smash her head against the screen until the machine broke and I could help myself to the money. I played my last dollar, which of course I immediately lost.

Debby moved efficiently, crushed my penis under her bulging buttocks, and then thrust her breasts into my face. She smelled of synthetic lavender perfume. She pressed my head between her sizable implants. It crossed my mind that it would be pretty great to be a dickhead at that moment. I wanted to share the joke, but I doubted she'd get my humour. She took advantage of our chat to settle accounts. *The song's ending, handsome, you've already had four dances, want me to carry on?*

Go ahead, beautiful, I want to get my money's worth. I turned her around and made her sit down again on my penis, hoping she'd hold the pose long enough to relieve me. Once the song was over, she assured me that although she was burning with an ardent desire to carry on dancing for me, I had to pay her now. *Don't you trust me, Debby?*

Yes, my petal, I trust you, but when you get to fifty bucks you pay, that's the rule. Fifty dollars for fifteen minutes, dancers are very dear people. She wavered between fake infatuation and hard business.

This comedy had gone on long enough. I pretended to look in my pockets. *The rest of my cash is in the car. I'll be right back.*

No fucking way, you're staying here! The atmosphere had suddenly changed. Debby wasn't wavering at all anymore.

Don't panic, I'm just going to my car and then I'll come back and get you to dance some more, you'll see, I'm nowhere near broke. She stared right at me. Her brown eyes were adorned with contacts that were supposed to turn them azure blue. *Don't move from this booth, I'll be back!*

As soon as she stepped out of the cubicle I followed her. She went straight to the security guy, a hefty gym rat and enthusiastic user of creatine and muscle stimulants. To my great joy, he was at the bar chatting with the waitress. A good distance away. I ran toward the exit. The bouncer took off at the same moment, without even knowing Debby's gripes. His instinct told him that a customer running away from the premises must have done something wrong.

I hurtled down the stairs and plunged toward safety. Just behind me I heard the door slam against the wall. I wouldn't have time to cross the road and get in my car. I decided to run behind the building but I regretted it immediately: I was trapped. He wouldn't have dared beat me up in the middle of the street. Too late. I could hear his footsteps right behind me. The brute hadn't just trained his biceps and pecs. He caught me and laid me flat on the ground with a powerful punch to my neck. I slumped onto the asphalt, turning round to take the blows head on. *Not the ribs, not the ribs. MMMPPFF!* The ribs.

He turned out to be good at sharing the love around, and covered almost all of my body. He went through my pockets, taking my cigarettes and lighter as well as a fake ID card. The swindled dancer joined him and laid into me with insults. Grabbing my hair in his fist, the bouncer informed me that I'd have to reimburse Debby before midnight as well as giving them a hundred dollars each for their trouble. He held out the ID card with a big grin. He was going to keep it as a guarantee. If I didn't come back that evening, he'd be paying me a visit with a few buddies and a few bullets. I promised him I'd be back the same evening to pay off my debt. What an idiot, too stupid to notice that the address was in Sainte-Foy.

I was planning on staying stretched out on the ground for a few minutes, assessing the damage before going home for the night to recuperate. I was about to get up when someone moved toward me. Shit, was he going to punch me again? I lifted my head. Two police officers. What a day.

Why won't you make a complaint? We can get a restraining order. It's the best way of ensuring your safety. He'll know we've got an eye on him. You're not the first person that gorilla's beaten up.

I nodded politely and let Sgt. Émond go on spouting his hogwash. He argued every which way, trying to convince me to press charges against the bouncer, or at least to formally identify him. *We received a call from a downtown resident. He saw everything, we know this guy who roughed you up. Can you at least corroborate the information?*

No. I'm sorry. I'd just gone outside for a piss when someone jumped me from behind. I didn't see anything, officer. I stuck doggedly to my version. There's only one possible approach with the pigs: wholesale denial. Deny everything, all the time. It's up to the lawyers to clear up all the inconsistencies and disprove the evidence.

You could have taken a leak in the bar, we know you were there.

No I wasn't.

Yes you were.

No, sir.

The atmosphere was heating up. Sgt. Émond slammed both fists on the interrogation table and glared at me over his trendy little glasses. He was as muscular as my attacker, and his forearm was covered in tattoos. I was impressed.

You don't impress me, officer.

Fuck! I don't know who you are or what your game is, but this is a bad idea.

What?

What what?

What's a bad idea?

Getting on my nerves, asshole! Don't move, I'm going to check if we were able to confirm your identity. I'll be back!

I was really proud of myself, I was taking charge of the interrogation like a real mafioso. I was sweating, I was trembling, but I was still handling the situation. Denying everything and protecting my identity were my guiding principles. I couldn't collaborate with the police. *You talk and you're done*, Mesrine would say. Everything gets out. And they file reports too, the bastards. They record everything in writing. If I wanted to have any chance of getting into the mafia or a reputable gang, my record had to be unblemished.

I felt like they gave me a proper grilling. They even left

me to stew for a bit. More than an hour sitting around in the interrogation room. I congratulated myself on having left the pills and the pot in my car. The dogs of the state search even the victims now: they made me take off my socks and ran a finger under the elastic of my pants. Isn't justice beautiful!

I scratched at the dried blood in my nostrils and ear. The barbarian doorman had ripped off a bit of my lobe. Well, not exactly ripped off, but torn. Knowing they were watching me through the two-way mirror, I took stock of the situation. The situation being my body. The wounds were superficial. They'd barely leave a scar. Scars suited me. They gave me character. The real issue was that he'd popped my ribs again, on the same side as the Saint-Agapit baseball team had. Now I'd have to sleep on my left side for a few more weeks. My ankle was messed up too. I already walked like a gangster but now I was seriously limping.

Alright, Mr. Comedian. We tracked down an SPCA employee who confirmed your name and faxed us your diploma. But we haven't got a photo to check. So we're going to take one. I have the feeling we're going to meet again. I'd like to keep it as a souvenir.

If this is how they treat the victims in Sherbooke, I think I'd rather be arrested somewhere else. Although ideally I wouldn't get arrested at all.

We're obviously going to see him again, we'll be keeping an eye out for him. His colleague leaning against the door frame had crossed his arms to make his muscles bulge. The Sherbrooke pigs must have a bodybuilding program. I thought he was pathetic, like a character from a bad film. Muscles are no use. You have to hit first, hit from behind, and be done with it. I should know.

Do it quickly, please. I ought to have refused or asked to talk to a legal-aid lawyer. I was too tired, I hurt too much, and desperately wanted a cigarette. And a joint. And some speed. And eight beers.

Stop squinting.

I'm not squinting. Some criminal masterminds manage to pose for a dozen different mug shots without looking the same twice. I was off to a bad start.

We're not going to wait all night for you to finish your clown act. Stop squinting or you'll be getting stuck like that. This photo's going to look like you one way or another. His comment had a great effect on his colleague, who creased up while groping his biceps. Very Burt Reynolds.

I stopped messing around, let them get my picture, and left the police station. They told me they were obliged to drive me back if I wanted, but I refused. I decided to walk downtown, slowly. We'd already wasted too much time together. It would have been pretty moronic if they'd taken me back to my car only to find out I was driving without a licence.

12

PATIENCE

This beating didn't fuck me up as bad as those two guys with sticks in Saint-Agapit, but I was still pretty messed up and barely fit to be seen in public. A black eye on the right side and a nice grazed patch on my left eyebrow. The savage had scraped my face on the asphalt. He'd be getting one of the top spots on my revenge list. Along with the arrogant pigs I'd just left.

The return trip was dragging, just like my foot, whose every step took enormous effort to lift off the ground. I had nothing to smoke, I was in pain, and I was alone. It's at times like this a guy wants to be with his mother. Or his grandmother. Or a sister or a female friend. Someone who'll be moved by our suffering and take care of us. Anyone.

I wanted Mama to forgive me for this new setback in our reunion so I picked a bouquet of red and white flowers from a municipal flowerbed. I tied them together with a fern stem and left them on her doorstep. I imagined her astonished face when she discovered my gorgeous arrangement.

I didn't want to sleep, I didn't want to go home, but I could hardly cruise around town all night. My favourite police officers might still be on the prowl. I barely had any gas left. I drank the last stolen can as I drove around the neighbourhood. I felt weird. The world was big, too big. Too many things could happen to me. This idea of infinite possibility, which might have energized me under normal circumstances, depressed me that evening.

I couldn't drop off. I was so full of resentment I'd have slept with my fists clenched, ready to punch. So I stroked myself violently. Whenever I stopped, a lump appeared in my throat. In the morning my penis was in worse shape than my face. But I still had to show up at work. At least I'd see Reynald and get to talk. After a long shower I applied some zinc cream.

Going to work was a good idea. It improved my morale and my budget. You'd never think a job had so many benefits in addition to the regular income. *Work is freedom*, declared Chaplin, a comedian.

I had a welcome committee waiting for me. The four female employees hurried over to me. Usually they ignored me or tossed out a quick greeting with a mild air of disdain. But that day they bombarded me with questions, tilting their heads to get a better angle on my wounds. I even detected some concern. Incredible. I was injured when they hired me too, but nobody made a big deal about my state then. I guess novelty is interesting. Maybe they'd started getting fond of me and were worried about my health.

I told them the whole story, right down to the tiniest detail. *I was on my way to volunteer at the Salvation Army, you know the place, on Wellington Street...*

Yes, yes, they knew where it was.

As I was walking there I heard someone crying for help. A young woman, a plump Hispanic, was signalling for me to go behind the building with her because her son had fallen and injured himself. Naturally I ran. I explained that I felt obliged to help the child since I was trained in first aid. *It was my duty.* With one voice they all approved. It was arousing to see them hanging off my every word.

I took up the tale again, inhaling the mix of cheap perfumes recently applied to necks. Women smell strong in the morning. *So I'd barely turned the corner when I saw three giants waiting for me. With sticks. Three big black guys.* They all nodded along with me.

Before I could dodge one blow, dozens of them were raining down on me. Even the Hispanic woman kept kicking me. That last detail had its intended effect. Lucie, one of the vets, put her hand on my shoulder, *Really brave, what you did.* I puffed out my chest. They told me I ought to have taken some time off to rest, that I looked exhausted. *No, I'm fine to do my job.* What a man I was.

When Reynald got there we figured out our tasks for the day and set off in the truck. Unlike the women, he didn't ask any questions, contenting himself with saying that he was there if I wanted to talk. He did say that it was valiant of me to have come to work with my injuries.

Even though he didn't interrogate me, I knew his curiosity was seriously aroused. I told him my story again, emphasizing the Hispanic woman's big chest and the Afro-Americans' brutality. My story was getting more refined with each reconstruction. Reynald let out some heartfelt onomatopoeias at the juicy parts, and didn't interrupt me until we'd arrived at our destination. We had to pick up two cats from an old woman who was going into a home.

It's crazy, seeing so much violence in a pretty town like this.

I reminded him that violence reigns everywhere, even in the remotest of villages. Even in Saint-Agapit!

We each took a cage. We took turns knocking on the door. We were about to leave when she answered it. It took considerable effort not to burst out laughing. The woman was made up like a drunken penguin who'd stumbled on a packet of felt-tip pens. Lipstick extended out over her cheeks on a face whitened with powder. Batman could easily have mistaken her for his worst enemy. Poor granny, her days of beauty were far behind her. Right back there with her dexterity.

Oh my God! Frozen on the doorstep, she couldn't take her eyes off me. *Have you seen what you look like?* I didn't dare utter the words I was thinking, but I pretended to be annoyed as I gave Reynald a sidelong glance.

It's nothing, ma'am, he had an accident. May we come in? We've come to pick up your little kitties.

Oh my God… She pressed herself against the door frame to let us pass, still repeating her litany, still staring at my face. She must never have seen an injured man before; she was more amazed than a slumdog on a catwalk.

Are you alone, Mrs. Gagné? She didn't answer Reynald, but he told me her son was supposed to be there. *I'm going to stay with you while my colleague goes to look for your cats, okay?* Good idea, dear Reynald, I'm going to look for the cats—among other things. *Do you know where your cats are, ma'am?* Radio silence.

With a nod I indicated that I was setting off on my mission. Armed with the first cage, I left them in the kitchen and walked toward the living room. I called out to the beasts and shook a box of treats, but nothing happened. After some slow, laborious contortions, I managed to crouch down and spot one under the buffet. I hadn't spotted anything particularly interesting on the buffet. Pressed against the heater, the creature thought it was out of reach. It was forgetting the tail at the end of its body. I dragged the cat out in one swift movement. It shouldn't have gripped the carpet. The pull drew out one claw and an unbearable yowl. A cat's cry is very human.

Everything okay in the living room?

I reassured Reynald. *Everything's under control, we've just got a delicate kitty on our hands.* The paw was bleeding as much as the cat was wailing. I grabbed its mouth and held it shut for a few seconds so it would get the message. The remaining claws tried to grip my gloves in vain. I swung it into the back of the first cage and picked up the second, determined to keep going.

Reynald was using his soft-as-honey voice to cajole Granny Makeup. I walked past them, flashed them a swollen-lipped smile that scared the old woman, and went into the bedroom. Jewellery box at three o'clock! I went right to it without hesitating, but it was locked. Since when do grannies lock jewellery boxes in their own houses? The box was too big for me to hide and sneak out. I couldn't force the lock or the lid. Fucking good quality wood! I had to silently find the key. The kitchen was very close by.

I was rummaging through the underwear when I heard a door opening. I jumped. It was the front door. *Mom, are you there?* The son, of course.

I quickly closed the drawer while Reynald introduced himself. The son explained that he was bringing boxes to pack his mother's things, that she had Alzheimer's and was getting more and more disorientated. No kidding.

I introduced myself in turn, announcing that I was going to look for the cat in the other bedroom. The son told me it would be in the basement, its favourite place, and went with me. We found the feline sleeping on a couch from another era. Black all over, with a white spot at the tip of its tail. He picked it up with one hand, stroked it with the other, and then put it in the cage. Quick look around. Nope, nothing interesting in the basement. I was leaving empty-handed, but buoyed by the thought of coming back for the jewellery box that same evening.

Reynald believed me that the first kitty had hurt itself in the cage. He didn't ask any questions since he was all emotional over the old lady wanting to stroke her cats through the bars of the cage. She whimpered and didn't want to let them go.

Reynald was overwhelmed. This lady reminded him of his own mother, who was also very sweet. She'd passed on two years ago after a long illness and multiple hospitalizations. It was painful, but I didn't listen to him all the way through. Reynald was on the verge of tears, right on the verge, but he didn't give in. To my great relief.

I took advantage of the fact that his heart was all gooey to remind him of my thrashing the day before. I reassured him that the physical consequences were tolerable. *I was made strong,* as Louis Cyr said. The main problem was that all my money had been stolen. I hadn't even had time to buy groceries. I had nothing left in my fridge or my pockets. I might be able to delay paying the rent, but I had to eat, *Do you understand, Reynald?*

Reynald was sorry but he didn't offer anything. I thought that was pretty cheap. Since I couldn't get him to do it, I had to make the offer myself. *It would be really helpful if you could give me back the money I gave you yesterday. I'll reimburse you when I get paid, along with my next repayment.*

He handed over the notes without smiling. At least I could down a few beers at the end of the day before paying a visit to Granny Makeup. There was no denying it, Reynald was a decent guy.

Those late-afternoon quiz shows are all interchangeable. It's always the same Z-list celebs with the same haircuts and the same complicit smiles on their faces, all excited about being there. The teasing hosts steal our time as they drag out the fake suspense for tacky prizes. After suffering through a whole game show thinking about this, I turned off the TV. I took my mind off things manually by opening my fifth can. I was drinking quickly. Too quickly, perhaps. It made me critical.

An intense burst of heat burned my face. And my individual portion of shepherd's pie wrapped in its aluminium container wasn't even ready. I'd scorched myself for nothing. I was impatient, and the empty feeling from the good old days was trying to settle in. I needed to move around. The basement damp was draining me. The stabbing pains in my ribs and nose were draining me. My desperate thirst was draining me. And I was getting restless.

I gobbled down the shepherd's pie slop in lukewarm mouthfuls. I put my gloves, the screwdriver, and my three remaining cans in my bag and set off on an adventure to the public library. The show must go on!

I sat down in front of computer station number seven, my lucky number. On either side, immigrant women looking for jobs. Gonzalezes, judging by their appearance. You poor women, start by inventing a resumé. Or do the same thing the rest of them do, go and clean rich people's houses, you can help yourself to the cutlery. Or better still, stay at home and have children. Apparently after the third one you make a profit. I wasn't short of an idea or two, I could have become an immigration counsellor.

Marie-Josée hadn't skimped on the threatening and insulting emails. I skimmed through a few, amused by her taste for the formulaic. *I'm going to bleed you and stuff you're body with bleech.* Tasty. *I'm gunna fuck you up the ass with a stick of brocken glass.* Original. *I'm gunna kick your head with high heals for every cent you stol from my ant.* A sporty project, how inspiring. And the best one: *I'm gunna stuf you're little dick down your throte with a durty plunger from the maul.* That was complete nonsense; I don't have a little dick.

The language is in a desperate state among barmaids and other drug addicts. The government ought to come up with some program. Put reminders of grammar rules on cigarette packages maybe. It's not like the rotten teeth and the cancer photos put anyone off.

Apart from that, still just as many women from Côte

d'Ivoire wanting to marry me, even some heiresses wanting to share their loot with me in euros. That scam really should have been Americanized by now. I moved quickly on to my dating sites' inboxes.

A striking number of lonely little pussies lived in Sherbrooke. All I had to do was update my place of residence to send the females flooding into my inbox. It wasn't a photo of me but the guy did actually look a bit like me. If we got to the meeting-up stage I'd explain to them that what with the boxing and everything I'd changed a bit. The information wasn't up to date either, but deep down nobody really reveals themselves. Ever.

I cast out a few lines to the least ugly, the biggest chests, and the most eager, suggesting dates that week. I was owed, I felt stressed. I lingered over the photos of the ladies in the hope of making out real breasts underneath blouses and camisoles. I've got nothing against fake tits, quite the opposite, *bigger is better*, as Lola Ferrari—a well-rounded woman—used to say. What upsets me is padded bras and other tricks that make scrawny chests look like generous bosoms. It kills me. It really ought to be illegal, under penalty of implants.

I was thinking about this when I had my first reply, a tall, pretty, blond trout wriggling on the end of my line. She wanted to chat. Ah, chat, that preliminary of preliminaries. Yes, I was new in the neighbourhood. Yes, I was looking for love, and no, I didn't have any children. Yes, yes. No, no.

Are you looking for something serious? I could feel her quivering over her keyboard.

I've had some difficult relationships, I'm looking for a healthy and straightforward love. No kidding, sweetie.

It must be a sign, I was going to write the same thing. I'd love to meet you, I feel like I can trust you, Mandy. It's important to call women by their name, then they feel unique. You might have slept with half the town, or even be a porn star, but you've got as much chance as anyone else if the girl feels unique.

You're unique, Mandy.

You don't waste any time.

I've wasted too much time waiting for you. Hurray for afternoon drinking. My prose was on fire!

LOL… I could be free on Friday…maybe…

Bingo! All that was left was to reel in the catch and stun her. I arranged to meet her the following Friday at 9:00 p.m., so she'd have plenty of time to simmer during the day, meaning I'd get stuck with the bare minimum of necessary chit-chat. We were going to meet at Blah-blah, a bar-restaurant conducive to a little fondling, among other tactics designed to reassure the ladies.

I'd had time to score with this hot little blondie while my two Marias were still struggling with their job-hunting sites, the expressions on their faces calling to mind their ancestors when they met the conquistadors. I almost wanted to team up with them with the noble aim of burgling a place or two. Just to bail them out. They must have a few little Ernestos to feed, poor things. Then I quickly changed my mind. *People best make dirty money on their own,* Seneca reminds us. I left them to their misery and, perked up by the possibility of a nice date, I decided to stop by the toilets. I went past the Quebec literature section. I'd spotted two promising novels by Nelly Arcan. I ripped off their covers.

13

RESPECT

The mobility my car gave me compensated for what I'd lost in terms of walking. It took me forever to limp over to my wheels, but once I was sitting down I could make the most of the great American engine. Powerful and noisy. I was gaining confidence, driving better and better, and thus faster and faster. Like everything else, you learn on the job.

I finished up my last can of beer, which was pretty warm by now, and took up my usual parking spot, two streets over from 1246 Prospect, the treasure chest where my mother sparkled. With difficulty, I dragged myself to my observation post. Mama was washing up. From the window where I was spying on her, I could see the whole of the living room and a good section of the kitchen. I was surprised not to see the bouquet I'd given her. I pressed myself up against the window, hoping to see it on the dining room table. But no. She must have been keeping it close to her, in her bedroom. I mean, it was a pretty attractive bouquet, nice and bushy.

The bearded guy was still on the scene, lingering around my mother's buttocks. He could at least let her work in peace. *The dishes won't wash themselves. Get yourself a dry towel and help her!* Telepathy maybe. Anything's possible. He followed my orders and carried out the task. Once it was completed, he left the apartment. Good boy!

We settled into our usual habits, and I watched, on a corner of the screen, an episode of some American series with Mama. She was nibbling on carrots with her homemade dip, ketchup and mayo mixed together. I promised myself I'd stop at the grocery store to steal the ingredients needed to taste this recipe. It would bring us closer together.

It was hard to keep up my crouched position with my pulped ankle as well as my stiff legs. I had to stand up often. That's probably what caught her attention. She came over to the window in a single bound. My heart nearly leapt out of my chest. Pressed against the outside wall, I saw her shadow on the cedar bush. She was looking for me. We hadn't been this close to one another for years.

I wanted to turn around and face her, but Mama might have screamed in surprise. Our reunion would have been wrecked. In love, you have to know when to hold back.

I gathered my wits by smoking one cigarette after another. Almost an hour later I was still shaking. That just shows what an effect my mother has on me. I drove around aimlessly, trying to pull myself together again. I even considered postponing the old lady's asset-stripping for a day or two, I was so upset. But you should never put off until the next day what you can steal that evening.

My daytime inspection had shown me that the basement looked like the best way of getting in. The windows were narrow but I'm slim. No dog, no alarm system. An entire house protected by a little plastic latch—pathetic. When I have my own house, I'll get an alarm system installed as soon as I move in. I'll have one put in at my mother's too.

I'm always hesitant to use my pocket flashlight, but the darkness made it necessary. Everything was already packed; cardboard boxes were strewn all around the big room. It was a burglar's Christmas. I opened a few boxes, finding nothing worthy of interest. I still took a collection of stamps that filled a large exercise book. Unlike people, old things sometimes get more valuable. I went up to the main floor. I'd come back for that wooden box. Something locked must contain a treasure. That's why women like mysterious men. I'm very mysterious.

I hoped the son had found a place for the old woman so the house would be empty. There was a dull noise. I stood frozen for a long minute. Clutching the banister, I could hear snoring. It was roaring like a Dynasty engine. Too powerful for a granny. The son was in the house. That complicated the entire operation. Especially with my smashed ankle: I wouldn't be able to take off if there were any problems. Too bad—nothing ventured, nothing gained. It's well documented. If the offspring had the bad idea of waking up, I'd threaten him with the screwdriver. And if he had the very bad idea of attacking me, I'd execute my threat—and him. Legitimate defence. It's a risk of the job.

I passed by the room I hadn't been able to inspect before. The rumblings were coming from in there. The door of the old dame's bedroom was half-open. I went in carefully. I headed toward the dresser and found the box, the object of my desire. I grabbed it straightaway. Turning round, I thought I might die. Or that I was already dead, for sure.

The old lady was staring at me. Two big white marbles bored right into my eyes. Sitting at an angle, leaning against three or four pillows, she was facing me. I leaned on the dresser so I wouldn't topple over backwards. A thousand hypotheses travelled through my mind like lost bullets. She was going to shout. I needed to get out through her bedroom window. I needed to jump on her and stop her from screaming. The son would recognize me and run for help. And nine hundred and ninety-six other things. This lasted a moment. Long enough for me to realize she wasn't blinking. I went closer and waved a hand in front of her face. Nothing. What a relief, she was dead. I got my breath back and removed the gold chain from around her neck.

I was face to face with my first corpse. It was cleaner than the next one. I thought about death as I looked at it. I was thinking about how much it changes the body before realizing that I didn't recognize her because her makeup was off. I closed her eyes and then opened them again. I checked to see if she had any gold teeth, then left her alone. Rest in peace, ma'am.

As I went past the other bedroom, I said to myself that Snorey needed to be warned. But the thought was inappropriate so I carried on, the little wooden box under my arm, soothed by the racket of the good son's sleep. He'd just saved himself a move.

I remember birthdays in the secure centres. I used to get a present decorated with a bow. Sometimes, when the social worker in charge of presents was a woman, there were colourful ribbon spirals around the bow. Men didn't bother with colourful ribbons. A card came with the present. The counsellors would scrawl a few morale-boosting words or some positive reinforcement. I preferred deeper reading material, so I quickly got rid of the card and moved on to excitedly unwrapping the present. Every time I was disappointed. I'd get underwear, watches, pencil cases. All practical stuff. What kind of present is that? A present should be something luxurious, something unexpected, something frivolous. What use is a useful present?

Granny Makeup had been crazy for some time. Long enough to stuff her little wooden box with junk, cramming it with family photos, keys, a silk handkerchief, and some paper tissues, all used. The jackpot every burglar dreams of, right? Even the box wasn't worth anything anymore; I'd had to stab it with a screwdriver to get at the treasure inside. In frustration, I thought that a watch or some underwear would have been welcome.

The evening wasn't wasted. My stop at the library saved the day. I had a date with Mandy and a picture of Nelly Arcan in a corset. I went to sleep late. Or early, depending on your perspective.

You still look tired, young man. Do you want to tell me what you really do at night?

Well, you look like a desperate stocky old man, do you want to tell me what you're really doing with your life? I kept that reply to myself. I'm good at controlling my impulses. Instead I told him I'd been sleeping badly because of my multiple injuries. For good measure, I threw in a quick groan and clutched my ribs.

Look at that, good work well done. I didn't get what he was showing me as he pointed at the sky. Was he a creationist on top of everything else?

Seeing my confusion, he took a step backwards and introduced me to his star candidate represented by a placard of a grizzled old man on a blue background, along with the Parti Québécois logo. Reynald bragged that he and his team of volunteers had put up more than a hundred around town the day before. I got the impression that the number one hundred was vitally important to him, it was the number that would make a difference.

We're going to win this election. I didn't understand how he could spend—worse, waste—his time helping a man steal a job in a government that would change nothing in his life. Nor in anybody else's either. He must have had time to waste, poor Reynald.

He could even become a minister. We see him at the Ministry of the Environment. From what I understood of politics, I knew that this ministry was just an offshoot of the Ministry of Trade and Development. You'd just have to turn a blind eye to the drilling and the river reroutings.

They're recyclable, right, these plastic signs with your Minister of the Environment's big face on them? Tiredness was making me petulant.

Listen, young man, they have to stay up for a month, we can't be using cardboard signs here. His quick flare of excited patriotism had nearly fizzled out. Scowling, he kept his eyes on the road, letting the placards pass by without him.

I rubbed it in clumsily. *How many mugshots does it take to get one vote?*

Remind me, how many mugshots have you had taken? A low blow. He regretted it immediately and apologized. Too late. I played the wounded innocent and clutched my ribs again. We're strengthened by other people's mistakes.

The evening looked as though it was going to be as long and difficult as the day I'd spent giving Reynald the cold shoulder. After the incident with my mother at the window I didn't dare go back to see her. I really needed to go and burgle a house later that night. I needed to compensate for Granny's handkerchief box, but my heart wasn't in it. I drank slowly, stubbing out joints and cigarettes halfway through. I swallowed a third speed without too much hope.

I cut my arm with a steak knife. I hadn't done that since I was a teenager. I was actually slicing through the old scars. I had several on my forearms, especially my left one. That evening, I just did my biceps so that it wouldn't be visible at work. Self-mutilation doesn't make you look very professional.

I know there's something off in this behaviour, that it's self-destructive and everything, but it's so effective. The discomfort goes away faster than it came. I controlled my pain, the depth and length of the cuts. I was subject to abuse from nobody except myself. And it couldn't be that bad if sometimes it felt good. I tasted my blood with the tip of my tongue right from the blade. It was salty and hot.

Three hours going round in circles in the basement. From the joint to the game console. From the toilets to magazines. From food to beer. From the knife to the joint. From the console to the pill to the knife and the last beer. At the beginning of the evening, I was shitfaced, worn out with boredom, stretched out on the bed waiting for the moment to spring into action.

I really hadn't expected Snorey to be at the house. Now that his mother was dead he could cry over her for a few days before slipping back into his usual routine again. All the grieving people I've ever met weren't grieving enough for my liking. When someone close to you dies, you should die too, a little at least.

I don't read women's magazines, but I know that between recipes it's all family, family, family. Surveys on the topic abound. Family must be in the top three personal values, along with money for anyone who's honest. Family comes across better, it's a beautiful value. The most zealous people even tattoo matchstick families on their vehicles. *It's important, it's the most precious thing I have, I could lose anything except my family*, my ass!

Parents serially divorce without giving a shit about their children. So we end up with blended families, who cares whether the different parts are compatible? And the old people, the elders, nobody gives a toss about them. People park them in homes like babies.

And we can't even be bothered to spread this supposed love for family to more than one generation, two at most. If you go as far as the grandparents, you're doing well. We don't know the names of our great-grandparents even though we're descended from hundreds if not thousands of generations before us. People aren't interested. The Vietnamese make little altars to their ancestors, but that's more about decoration than filial piety. The amphetamines were taking effect at last. My mind was agitated. My jaw too.

I swore to myself that as soon as I could question my mother I'd trace my genealogical tree back to its roots. I'd find out names, get hold of all the available photos of my ancestors, and put up an enormous family tree on my bedroom wall to feel close to my family, who would never leave me again, ever.

On my third pass in front of the late Granny Makeup's house, I parked. No sign of life, everything was turned off, just like its inhabitant. I kept telling myself I shouldn't have come back, I was getting soft.

Snorey was there for his mother, at least. That was something. I set off with the biggest strides my bashed-up body could manage. There were already some letters in the mailbox. I added the photographs, keys, and kleenex I'd found in the little box.

I'd given myself permission to throw away the used ones.

I stopped off at the convenience store long enough to swipe a half-litre of red. It was a crappy evening. I shouldn't have cut myself. I shouldn't have done so much speed. I shouldn't have gone to the old lady's place. I downed the wine and breathed through my nose as much as I could.

With all those *shouldn't have*s, I'd never get anything done. I swallowed the last mouthful, lit a butt, and got going. I had to get my head straight, starting with a nice little profitable burglary.

14

INTROSPECTION

I was turning into a real pussy. Being emotional is dangerous for a gangster like me. I was standing in the middle of the child's bedroom and admiring the collection of teddy bears on the bed. They were green, red, blue, mauve. Even pink. It was a bit gay for a boy's room. His parents must be intellectuals. Intellectual people are even more dangerous than emotional ones.

As a kid I used to have a stuffed rabbit. I called it Papa. The teachers thought that was a bit unhealthy so I had to call it Poppet. I called it Papa in secret. I lost it when I was little; I suppose it got left behind in one of the moves between families.

I got hold of myself and turned back to inspect the living room. An old stereo. Some CDs. Nobody uses those anymore. Even pawnbrokers won't take them. Worthless trinkets. Some alcohol, at least. Old people's alcohol, rum from holidays, pink tequila and crème de menthe. I took the lot. There's no such thing as a too-low alcohol content.

I picked up the change jar from under the parents' box spring. It was heavy and it made me move about like a scoliosis king, all twisted. My ribs were healing less quickly than they had the first time. With each new injury it takes longer to bounce back. I put the money jar, which I reckoned contained more than a hundred dollars, and the first load of alcohol on the back seat. There was still a lot of room left in the vehicle. I decided to go back and explore. Surely there must be some jewellery there, maybe some weapons I'd missed. It was a pleasant grey-brick bungalow. If I couldn't find anything else, it would mean they were a hypocritical family showing off above their means.

I started up my looting again. I discovered a few necklaces and men's rings. I also decided to keep a chain bracelet, which I put on then and there. I was just on the point of leaving when I lingered in the child's room again. He had a whole collection, he wouldn't notice a missing bear. I chose the white one with the red bowtie. I couldn't say why. I don't think it was for me. But I didn't have anyone to give it to. Maybe my mother, if she liked teddy bears. I set it down beside me on the passenger seat. I fastened its seat belt and declared its name Co-pilot.

I appreciated burglary with a car. You could take more stuff and get away faster. I glimpsed a world of possibilities driving along the highway. I whistled the tune from *Space Pirate Captain Harlock* as I headed off into the night.

Now it was Reynald's turn to give me the cold shoulder. He must have read one of the day's newspapers. The headlines were giving his future minister protegé some difficulties. Yet another corruption scandal, some tale of an illegally financed campaign. No kidding! They all do it. Everyone's equally pathetic. You have to take that for granted and move on. It's like doping and competitive cyclists, like speed for truck drivers. *It's in the game*, as Ben Johnson whined.

The need to talk is often stronger than the need to ignore someone. Buddhism and sulking both require silence and a concentration out of reach of most ordinary mortals. Reynald was very ordinary and very mortal. *They haven't even got proof, they just ask the question and he's already condemned.* He was boiling with rage.

Yeah, Reynald, you're right, it's not fair. It was time to make up.

Now try telling me that the papers don't take sides. They do take sides, they take the Liberals' side! Reynald was on fire; I was afraid he would turn to face me. The old activist spat way too much when he was excited. It was all over the dashboard.

You're absolutely right, Reynald. Seeing a journalistic conspiracy in it seemed exaggerated to me, but I was trying to repair our collapsed bridges. When broken bones calcify, it often makes that part of the bone more solid. Soon my ribs would be stronger than rock. I thought the reunion with my mother would make us a more bonded family as well, that the years of separation would take nothing away, would even increase the strength of our relationship. It was a morning for big analogies.

You're on another planet, young man, what are you thinking about? Reynald was looking closely at me. I had no need to be afraid of missiles. He was waiting for a reply.

You're right, I'm often on another planet, sometimes I even get all the way to Saturn. We chuckled—I've got a knack for making fun of myself when necessary.

So, what were you thinking about, astronaut? He was persistent, the old sovereigntist. I refrained from filling him in on my reflections on the state of my body and my family. Instead I switched to our eating habits, which we'd be needing to change.

We always eat sandwiches from the dep. I've found a good restaurant that specializes in breakfast and lunch. We could stop there at lunchtime? He agreed without much conviction. We were going to eat at Mama's restaurant. I started sweating right away.

No lineup that day. It was an omen. My mother came to greet us and told us to follow her. To the end of the world, Mama. I let

Reynald have the banquette seat. Bad move. My little wooden chair gave me a less panoramic view of the whole restaurant. I even lost sight of my mother, and then jumped when she appeared at our table. I was so happy to see her again that I was sweating and trembling like anything. Reynald put it down to my fourth coffee, advising me to cut down on the amount of caffeine I consumed. My poor Reynald, if only you knew everything that's been through my body. I can take it.

I wanted to eat a ham omelette with a side of hash browns. But go figure, I couldn't get the words out. My mother was so beautiful and smiling that I was losing my cool, which I have a lot of. I was really stammering. After the third attempt, I said, *A worker's special!* without stumbling. The brain is a crazy thing.

As soon as she'd gone back to the kitchen to give our order, Reynald started teasing me. *You like them old, young man.*

It was in bad taste. I pointed out that she was a very beautiful woman but I wasn't interested in her that way.

In what way then? Reynald was definitely going for a spot on my list of terrible revenge. I changed the subject, got him talking about cars. They'd announced an exhibition of vintage automobiles in Jacques-Cartier Park. Reynald didn't yet have a vehicle prestigious enough to show, but he was saving so he could be in the next one. Old men remembering the good old days while admiring each other's old cars. I showed an exaggerated interest.

By that point in the day, I only had half an amphetamine in my body, so my appetite was pretty good. The food was too. Drowning in maple syrup it was better still. Mama noticed, revealing that she too loved maple syrup. I had tears in my eyes at that. Of course you love it! I had a thousand replies and even more questions, but I stayed stunned in my chair, my face even more strained than my heart. That's saying something. Reynald saved my skin, putting forward a hypothesis about a conspiracy between dentists and Quebec's maple-syrup producers. My mother thought he was funny, I was jealous.

As we left, Mama asked me how I'd got hurt. She was a real mother, my mother. I reassured her, stammering that the marks on my face would fade sooner than she might think. I had to admit that the ankle was hardly getting better. *Yes, yes, I-I've s-seen a d-doctor.* I would have grabbed her and squeezed her in my arms. Hard enough to break my ribs again. But we had to leave. Just as if nothing was up.

In the truck, tension flared up again between Reynald and me. He thought I was weird for leaving a twenty-dollar tip for a ten-buck lunch. I retorted that the service was exceptional and that I could do what I wanted with my money. In a fit of meanness, he suggested that I could also repay my debt to him, in that case. The day continued in the silence of Rouge FM.

I was very tense that evening. The ups and downs in my relationship with Reynald, coupled with meeting my mother at the restaurant, added to the stress of the first date. I knew nothing about Mandy, so I had few expectations, but still, it could be love. And who knew if I'd manage to fuck her; I didn't know what kids were like in the Eastern Townships. It'd already been a big day, and the evening looked like it would be pretty hefty too.

Mandy and my mother took up all my thoughts in the shower. I washed myself vigorously, careful to clean everywhere. As I dried my hair I looked for my mother's features in the mirror. The smile, maybe. And the neck, we both had very slender necks. A sign of nobility. I didn't skimp on the cologne, applying it all over my skin. I thought I looked good. Good like my mother. Remembering her concern for my injuries and her enormous smile when I left the restaurant, I decided I ought to make the most of that situation.

I'd go and meet her that week.

The wait had gone on long enough.

With a light heart and a head full of joy, I set off for Blah-blah. I arrived a few carefully calculated minutes late. It's essential to let women stew. They need a scene to be set, a bit of resistance, and some mystery to open their heart—and their thighs along the way. Mandy was wearing the same black dress she'd had on in several photos on the site. It really was her. Good, she'd showed herself to be honest.

I sat down opposite her and savoured the effect of the surprise. She seemed disturbed, even looking round for help. I reassured her right away, it really was me. The difference from the photos could be explained by the professional boxing I was doing, and the angle and light of the shot, but it really was me. *Disappointed?* No, of course she wasn't.

I'm just surprised, you really don't look like you at all.

The important thing is that we're together and having a good time. You have nice features, Mandy.

Oh, okay. Thanks. She was shy. Girls play at that. They like to think it's charming. In all chick flicks, the heroine is an awkward ingenue. Chick flicks really mould their personalities.

I began the conquest with the old proven strategy of interest. I asked her a ton of questions about her work, her life, her passions. I didn't stop.

Cats? I love cats, I have three. Three's a good number, believable.

While I wasn't listening to her tell me about her cats, I noticed a tattoo on her right wrist, very discreet, in cursive letters. I grabbed her hand, which was damp and cold. That was a good sign, I was having an effect on her. I brought her wrist up to my eyes and read in a whisper: *Believe.* We were made to get along; I had dreams to spare.

When I thought she felt unique, and trying hard not to ogle her breasts too much, I told her about myself. I talked about boxing, investment management, computers. Geniuses can be identified by their spontaneity. I told her that I'd invented the term *LOL*. She was skeptical, even saying that it astonished her or, rather, that it would astonish her. I told her that when I was a programmer at Apple I used a lot of acronyms to simplify communication. I was known for this habit in the computing world.

Over time, I noticed that LOL, laughing out loud, in case you didn't know the original meaning, had escaped from me. I started finding it everywhere online. Of course, I couldn't copyright it, but it's flattering to know I've contributed to the development of information communication. She seemed less impressed than I'd hoped.

We were on our sixth beverage, two for her, four against me. The gap was widening even though I was stretching out the time between sips. I know girls sometimes confuse good drinkers with alcoholics. Everyone likes good drinkers. Women don't like alcoholics. I waited for her to finally finish the last gulp of her Bloody Mary before I ordered again.

When you say you want a serious relationship, did you mean exclusive?

I didn't understand what the question meant.

She clarified. *I'm looking for something serious, but also for fun. I don't think we're seriously clicking here. But if you want, we can go home together, no strings attached.*

Wow, she was a saint! We'd go right up to seventh heaven without having to use all those rusty old commitment keys. I'd been through that whole spiel for nothing. I confirmed that her perspective on relationships suited me perfectly and I insisted on continuing the evening at her place. *My cleaning lady's on maternity leave, my place is too much of a shithole, my cats can be funny*, and so on and so on.

I was to meet her at her place. The directions were straightforward. I was impatient to get back to her but I drove under the limit. I wanted to make sure she wouldn't see my car, it might contrast with my programmer talk. The delay would also give her time to put on some kind of end-of-evening outfit, in black or red lace, and to carry out her intimate grooming. Women are particular about that. I personally prefer the aroma of a long day that invades your nostrils and stings your eyelids, but women these days are shy about their little sugar plums.

I'd dawdled on the way for absolutely no reason. She was waiting for me in the parking lot. No outfit nor clean sugar plum on the program this evening. We kissed and felt each other up leaning on her car, an Acura, a girls' car. She pulled me toward the building and insisted we had to be silent at all costs. The apartment walls were cardboard and she had a tricky relationship with her roommate. That got me excited. I was fantasizing that if we orgasmed at top volume, the roomie might come and join in.

Her apartment was in the corner of the fourth floor. Inaccessible from the outside. Shame. It was home to a lot of valuable items.

Crossing the living room, I whacked my toe on a low table. Mandy burst out laughing, pulling me by the hand toward her bedroom. Once the door was closed, I thought she'd put a light on, or at least a candle. Grabbing my waist in the darkness she tipped me over onto the bed. She kissed me with a lot of passion and a lot of tongue. I didn't want to break her momentum but I suggested turning a light on. *I'm a visual person, see?* She replied in the negative, busily licking away like a cocker spaniel.

For men, one of the downsides of unlimited access to pornography is the expectation of seeing. *Not that there's anything wrong with that*, said Jerry Seinfeld in a different time. Men's retinas have never, in the entire history of humanity, been so bombarded with naked women being penetrated every which way. Sight has become a sex organ. I couldn't really see myself explaining that to Mandy. I told myself that she must have her reasons, she must have deformed nipples or something like that.

I reluctantly agreed to carry on in the dark.

Tangled up in our last few pieces of clothing, I was just about to discover her interior beauty when she handed me a condom, that great passion killer. I murmured that we didn't need one and tried to gently force my way in. She insisted that it was the condom or nothing. I reassured her that I'd only ever had one girlfriend, with whom I'd lost my virginity two years before. She thought this confession was cute and let me go about my little business.

It was a pious lie. I was sure we'd both be winners here, at least in terms of pleasure. And genital herpes doesn't get transmitted every time, especially if you're asymptomatic like me.

In the end the dark was good. In terms of atmosphere and performance. With the thrusts, the slapping of thighs, the slaps on buttocks, and the sighs, we woke up the roommate. She noisily clattered the dishes in the kitchen as I was making Mandy come. I'd performed well and held off for as long as possible. But as soon as I strangled her a bit, I couldn't hold back and I came inside her, gasping loudly.

I always keep an eye on the time when I'm fucking. We were pushing eight minutes, very close to my personal record. Mandy, no doubt satisfied, came back from the bathroom and offered me a SpongeBob SquarePants towel. I made a joke imitating the character's voice, but she didn't laugh. I've noticed that women are often sulky after making love. It must be a hormone thing. She asked me to get dressed and leave. No, she wasn't up for another round, she'd had enough. Yes, it was good, thank you.

I set off, cigarette in my mouth. If it hadn't been for the pain in my ribs it would have been a perfect moment. I took the highway at top speed, the radio blasting, singing along with Christina Aguilera. *La la la la...*

The following morning I arrived at work with a sense of sexual fulfilment. The adventure hinted at a good week ahead, suggesting that the family reunion would also unfold without a hitch. You have to know how to read the signs. In this burst of joy, I even bought Reynald a coffee. A kind of peace pipe, a nice steaming potion. He accepted it but pointed out that I should be saving my pennies to pay him back. He was asking me to give him the two payments out of my next paycheque, no matter what came up. *One day at a time, Reynald, one day at a time. It's the secret of happiness.* He didn't seem convinced. He wanted his due. *Just watch me*, René Lévesque would have promised.

Even the coffee tasted of happiness that morning. It's always better in a paper cup. You don't even have to wash your mug, you just enjoy the coffee and throw the cup in the garbage. And if you can also sit in a big truck smoking cigarettes, that's the American dream. And if you're a man and if you're white, that's the dream of the whole planet.

Reynald laid out the day's plan for me. We'd clock up some miles: we had several animals to pick up in the surrounding villages, and medicines to be bought at two vet clinics. Nothing special. We'd start by rescuing a feral cat. Nobody knew how it had got in, but the cat was stuck in the roof of the house. So we needed to go to Bromptonville, a poor village.

On the road I talked about politics to make Reynald happy. He told me the tide was turning, the polls were once again favouring his candidate, they had to do everything possible to keep it that way until the election. With a great lucidity I didn't know he possessed about political affairs, he explained to me that in a democratic country like our own, everything was a question of image and trend above all else. Yes, all the candidates swung between fake fears and false promises, but the saddest thing was that they truly believed in their agenda. They couldn't explain it properly because the media treated everything as a sound bite. It seemed like a good moment to put in an ambiguous *Mmm-hmm.*

He resumed with even greater intensity. *And forget door-to-door. The majority of citizens don't even understand what system of government we have, let alone which level of government is involved in which decision.* Reynald was showing his true colours, especially red. His polarities were finally converging; he scowled passionately. He was getting carried away, we were close to his spitting point. I turned my face away.

Here we are, like idiots, wasting hours and hours volunteering to educate them, but they go and vote with their feelings, depending on the attractiveness of the tie, or the bus, what a load of crap.

I decided to swoop in and rescue him, and share a bit of philosophy at the same time. *In one of the foster families I lived with, there was this really decent guy, Réjean, a kind of modern sage who helped me understand life with one single sentence: Don't lie to yourself or get false hopes, most people are fat, ugly, and stupid. That still helps me understand humanity...* Reynald admitted that Réjean was a sage, but he didn't notice that he himself was a bit fat and not favoured in the features department. In his defence, I didn't think he was a total idiot.

We chatted for a moment in front of the house with the cat in the ceiling while we finished up our big coffees. We flipped a coin to decide who would climb up to haul out the kitty. Reynald wanted nothing to do with the queen, so I called heads and the caribou won.

The roof was stuffed with mineral wool. I'd scarcely got my head in the hole before I was itching from head to toe. It took me about ten minutes to track down the cat, hidden away in a corner under the insulation. It was skinny and trembling, so desperate that it let itself be picked up without even meowing. I could feel its ribs despite the thickness of my gloves. I stroked its head to calm it and hummed some Wu-Tang in its ear. I handed it to Reynald, who shut it in the cage. We decided to take it right back to the centre so that it could receive the best care. It must have been a special cat, with an indigo aura and everything. The idea of hurting it didn't even cross my mind, which is normally so quick.

15

JOIE DE VIVRE

At the end of the day, the sun was shining, and a breeze as soft as a baby's bum was blowing. It was pleasant so I decided to go for a walk, with the idea of strengthening my recovering ankle. Reynald recommended the Lake of Nations, a walk of a few kilometres, with lots of facilities, where all the local female runners wearing leggings would be on show. He went on about it being a feast for the eyes.

I'd kept on my work shirt with the SPCA logo. I hate men in uniform, whether they be police officers, prison wardens, or soldiers. Even convenience-store employees. But this uniform was different. It was a nice-guy uniform. Even though it was beige and brown I was convinced it would have an effect on the girls I passed. Everyone loves animals, even people who eat them and abandon them. A proud protector of these vulnerable creatures couldn't fail to provoke admiration.

I walked with my face to the sun, to tan a bit. I do have a pale complexion and had big purple bags under my eyes. Some people might call them suitcases; I was all set for a long trip. With a little bronzing, I'd be extra-handsome. My new scars would be shown off to advantage.

Although I caught several sly looks that were full of interest, I didn't meet anyone. I must have been emitting a scent of sex, some pheromones or whatever, that gave away my relations from the night before. Women like feeling unique and having exclusivity over the male they enslave. It's well documented. I smiled it off, not letting it diminish my happiness. The sun, the firm asses, and the lapping of the waves on the lake inspired me. I decided to go and meet my mother the next morning.

I couldn't sleep that night. The stress and the joy of the imminent reunion made my guts churn. I'd avoided drinking too much alcohol so that I could keep my breath fresh. I'd restricted myself to a single amphetamine during the day to help me sleep. All in vain. I had nothing left except for cigarettes and half a gram of hash to manage the anxiety and the joy. I smoked joints, some hash in a bottle, then did some hot knives. All evening and well into the night.

Morning started at 4:00 a.m. that day, I'd decided. It would give me time to get ready. Bad idea. I shaved three times, and all the last one achieved was cutting my chin. I had two showers but I still felt dirty. Sleepless nights are never spotless. And you're never clean enough to meet your mother.

She started her shift at six-thirty, as I'd noted the first time I shadowed her. I decided to knock on her door at twenty to six. That would be perfect. We'd have a few minutes to chat, hug each other tightly, and then she'd leave for the restaurant. It was reassuring to enclose this big moment in a controlled space of time. If I stammered or burst into tears, I wouldn't have to put up with the embarrassment for too long. It was just a first contact. We'd meet up again the same evening or the following day, happy.

I barely avoided accidents all the way there. Stress, tiredness, and happiness. I congratulated myself on not having drunk anything. I was less dangerous and I had fresh breath. I practised the intensity of my gaze in the rear-view mirror and the phrases I'd repeated a thousand times in a small voice, so as not to wear them out. *Mama, it's me, at last!... Hello, Mom, do you recognize me?... It really was me, I know you recognized me at the restaurant... Peek-a-boo, it's your little boy!* The suntan, more like a sunburn, minimized the appearance of the wounds on my face, which were already getting much better. Mama would be happy to see that, maybe even reassured. Out of habit, I parked two streets over and walked.

The distinctive feature of big moments is that they put all the little gestures into perspective. I hesitated in front of the door for a long time. Should I knock or ring? In the Bible, the prodigal son's return is announced. He was seen returning from a long way off. Nobody was announcing me anywhere. I rang, it felt more official.

The door half opened and a man appeared in the frame, his top half naked. He seemed annoyed. It took me a moment to recognize him but it was Mr. Fournier, my mother's lover and my potential father. He had as much beard on his chest as he did on his chin, which was fascinating. He repeated his question for the third or fourth time: *What do you want?*

What did I want? So many things, where to start? First I asked to speak to Marie-Madeleine, with a composure that amazed me. The man shut the door and left me waiting outside, alone with my thoughts. It's like with sex, it's best not to think about it too much, that moment of initial contact. It would get me all flustered. I needed to stay full of confidence, as I had with the hairy guy.

The door opened, revealing my mother, looking luminous. I hoped she might invite me in and welcome me into her space. She stayed in front of the door, turning round only to confirm to her boyfriend that it was indeed me, *the guy from the restaurant.* That revived my courage: she'd talked about me to people close to her, she'd already recognized me. I knew it!

I'm so happy to meet you at long last. I've been planning this for so long... I seemed to have left my oratorical talents in the car two streets away. A long silence fell, not to be mistaken for an awkward one. It was actually an emotional one.

Why did you come here, to my house? I don't even know you...

I sensed fear in her voice. She must have been afraid of my reproaches, after all these years, convinced that I resented her for having let social services kidnap me and imprison me far away from her. *I know, I know, I-I want us to g-get to know each other p-properly. For us to t-take up where we l-l-left off.* I tried to be reassuring.

She wasn't reassured. *There's no connection between us. How did you find me?*

I wanted to cry, leap into her arms and embrace her, whisper to her that everything was okay, that there was nothing wrong anymore. She was my mother. She'd finally recognized it; I had *found* her. The power of the verb. My years of reading confirmed it. One single sentence, one single word, can change everything. My heart filled with the word *found,* I stammered, a lump in my throat: *We still have t-t-time, we're go-going to get to know one another. You're right, we've f-found each other. That's the important thing.*

The man had put his big hairy hands on my mother's shoulders and was steering her inside. She repeated, *How did you find me?*

It seemed to me that this was an important technical detail for her. I couldn't tell her about Marie-Josée and Google, that wasn't very sophisticated. Neither was I going to admit that I'd been spying on her for the last two weeks, even if it was out of love. She might think I was weird. I opted for simplicity. *I r-recognized you and I followed you w-when you left the restaurant.*

That's what I thought.

I had the impression that she was talking to Mr. Hairy with this thought. The man who seemed increasingly unlikely to be my father. I found him disagreeable and less handsome than me. Too hairy. Not even ginger. And he wasn't letting go of my mother.

You seem like a nice kid, but I can't do anything for you. You should get help. There's lots of resources in Sherbrooke, you know. She took a step back. He was controlling her, it was clear. He must have been Greek, Greeks like to dominate.

B-b-but the only thing I need is you! I-I want us to talk, to talk a lot, to get to know each other, to watch t-television together while we eat spaghetti.

She froze. She'd understood. *Okay, this is too weird. I'm going to ask to you please leave. I've got to get ready for work. I'm sorry… You need to leave.*

She freed herself from old hairy with a twist of her shoulder and went back into her apartment without embracing me. He stayed there, glaring at me with his Greek guard-dog look. *Listen to me good, I don't know who you are or what you want, but I'm going to be very clear: don't ever come back here, or anywhere near here, or it's me you'll be dealing with.*

You're not my father! I smiled spitefully at him before turning on my heel.

At the wheel of my racing car I was flying like the wind. Whimpering with happiness between two sobs, I constantly repeated every word we'd exchanged so as not to forget anything. It hadn't gone quite as planned, but nothing ever goes as planned, except in wrestling. But the main thing was there. I'd found my mother, that much was confirmed. Our first contact hadn't been bad, reunion magic would kick in soon. With a knot in my throat, unable to free my voice, I was happy. Very. Maybe too happy. Maybe even way too happy.

I was feverishly gnawing my nails. My fingers were bleeding with happiness.

My bedroom was now the size of the universe, as enormous as the possibilities opening up to me, to both of us. My mother and me. The Greek would find himself out of the picture pretty damn quickly. Stretched out on the uncomfortable little mattress in my damp room, I revelled in the comfort of filial love and replayed the scene in my head in sepia.

Mama was in shock. I understood that, after all these years. I was too—and I'd been prepared, unlike her. Her heart and mind must have been very preoccupied at the restaurant. Maybe so much so that she would get orders wrong or pour coffee on the customers. I smiled.

I remembered every second of our encounter, avoiding the parts with the Greek, too unpleasant.

How did you find me? The key sentence, Pandora's question. She'd let this sentence slip out in a weak voice—no, a soft voice—to emphasize its meaning. She must have been impressed by my problem-solving and organizational abilities. She herself must have been looking for me for years. Where was her unease stemming from? Maybe because I'd been the one to bring the process to a close when this denouement was actually part of her role as mother. That was all it could be.

As a child, when I used to call the emergency services as I packed a hospital bag, the social workers judged that I was my mother's caregiver. What morons! And I'm not today either. Everyone in a family needs to take turns looking after each other. If they don't, there's nothing authentic, you're just stuck in your roles. It's meaningless. They must have made my mother feel guilty about everything she was unable to do at the time.

She'd asked me to leave, but I'd expected that. She needed to get ready for work, needed to put her makeup on again after having cried with all that emotion. It could be, too, that she hadn't been with the Greek for long, not long enough to reveal to him that she had a son. That used to happen when I was young too. Sons make men run away. It's well documented. One thing was clear: that maniac was not right for her. For her to ask me to leave was just about okay. But that son-of-a-gun ordering me never to return was unacceptable. *You're not even my father, you greaseball!* I was losing my temper; I tried to avoid thinking about him, but he took centre stage and imposed himself on the memory. He was spoiling the picture. I slotted him in at the top of my list of violent revenges to be carried out. That relaxed me and I took up the flow of my memories once more.

I was feverish, impatient to see her again. But Mama didn't know how to get hold of me. I would go and find her soon. *If the mountain won't come to you, go to the mountain,* said Lauren of Arabia, a Maghreb poetess. That was a good idea, the mountain part too. We could go for a family hike.

In the meantime, I had to stroke myself to calm down. I opened a memories file. Mandy's tongue came into my head, and into the palm of my hand.

Time had flown by like a shooting star. I arrived at the office just in time, avoiding another late start. Reynald smiled as he saw me run across the parking lot, tucking my shirt into my pants. *Calm down, young man, it's going to be a quiet day.*

He explained to me that they'd cancelled a rescue of dogs in Eastman but that we might have to go and catch an aggressive ferret in a primary school a few minutes away. I spared a thought for Bushy.

I took advantage of the lack of work to wander around the centre. The door of the cupboard where they kept medicines, darts, and other interesting products was always locked up tight. I checked, on principle. Everything was secured. I had access to medicines and darts in the truck, but Reynald kept scrupulous accounts. I wanted to spend some time in the toilets, but I was already irritated. Instead I went into the big room where we look after the dogs and cats destined for adoption and, ultimately, to be euthanized.

Most people felt assaulted by the cacophony in there. But it calmed me down every time. The hissing, meowing, yapping, and growling blocked out my thoughts. It rested me. It's not always easy having a quick mind like mine, it can get exhausting. I was thinking about the importance of breathing in life when I noticed Laura sitting on the ground. Laura was one of the least unpleasant employees. She was sitting at the end of a row of cat cages with a litter of kittens in her crossed legs.

I went up to her. She gestured to me to sit down next to her and handed me a kitten, black and grey, with blue eyes. It was cute, I have to admit. Bastards are good-looking in the animal kingdom. Among humans too, sometimes, but the stakes are different. If humans mix too much we're all going to be frizzy and brown, there won't be any blue-eyed blondes left. And it would be a shame not to have any really black black people around. Just mixed people with varying shades of skin. I'm all for interracial fucking, but let's leave it at that.

You seem miles away, what are you thinking about?
I think this kitten's a handsome mix.

Laura agreed, and started introducing the six little ones to me, according to the features of their fur and the colour of their irises. We named them as we went along. In the end, we had Gandalf, Minoune, Moumoune, Frimousse, Killer, and Jean-Pierre. Gandalf was the most magical. He meowed constantly, throwing us evil looks. His curses attracted his mother's attention. She was allowed to roam the room freely. She turned the corner yawning, seemed surprised at seeing us in the company of her litter, and immediately fled. Laura got up to bring her back. *The kittens must be hungry. We'll gather them together and leave them be.*

Laura had a delayed-action beauty. A hidden charm, heightened by nothing in particular. Like those women you need to see a few times before you realize they're beautiful. I was at this stage of observation, stirring up the idea of inviting her to get a drink and get laid. While I waited, I slipped one kitten and then two under my shirt. Their fur was soft. There was still room and I managed to grab Jean-Pierre. Laura appeared right then with the mother.

Ha ha! What are you doing? she'd laughed, which I thought was good. Women like to think they are unique, to have control and to laugh.

I'm developing a heating system based on kitties, you want to try it?

You remind me of Lenny.

Who?

Lenny, the Steinbeck character. You know him?

Oh, yes, I know the one. I hate people who think they're superior because they've seen a film before other people. If she wanted to play at intellectuals, she'd got the wrong number. I've read dictionaries, lady! *Have you read* The Alchemist *by Paulo Coelho?*

Yeah, Paulo Coelho, of course, why?

No reason, it's just a good philosophical book, that's all. Ha! I immediately felt as though I'd had the desired effect and set the record straight.

You're a special guy, you know?

Special enough to ask you out for a drink tonight? We could chat about movies. Hesitation is just a *no* waiting to be caressed. *Come on, I think it would be fun...*

I have a yoga class, but we could get together after. But for tea or coffee though. I don't drink alcohol.

Right. Double dose of amphetamines for me then. *You must*

be very supple. I caught a kitten that was threatening to escape.

Well, not that supple, no. Why?

The girls I've known who loved yoga were supple. You'll get there with practice. I'd never met a girl who did yoga, but that didn't mean I didn't know what I was talking about.

Okay, you really are different! You've got to put the kittens down now. It's lunchtime. Minoune, Killer, and Gandalf were already suckling their mother.

I sneaked one last kitten cuddle before letting them go off and join their siblings.

We'd retrieved the evil ferret, saved a raccoon stuck on a balcony, and discussed politics at length. Reynald let me go early. I found myself free in the middle of the afternoon. I had a few bills in my pocket. But I was going to need a top-up soon. That same night, or the next day, if I closed the deal with Laura that evening. I was keeping the night in reserve.

My desire to knock back some large beers at the first bar morphed into the leggings tour. Driving along the Lake of Nations, I noticed that it was packed. I decided to linger there.

I still really wanted a drink. I decided to solve that problem in the parking lot. I only know one way to get rid of the desire for alcohol, and that's by taking drugs. Knowing that my next engagement, conquering Laura, wasn't coming up for a few hours, I decided to spoil myself. Bad plan.

16

SENSITIVITY

The sun was fantastic, the asses it was toasting were even more so. To burn off the buzz from the pills and the energy drinks I'd downed during the day, I played a bit of Don't Lose Sight Of. This newly minted discipline consisted of running after all the female joggers with bulging buttock muscles on my path. What seemed like a good idea proved to be energy-guzzling. I'm pretty intense. After a dozen chases, I was sweating and spitting up my lungs in the form of little clots. When I stopped, on the verge of passing out, I realized that I'd bust my ankle again. You forget the importance of not running on a recovering ankle.

I was dragging my foot toward my car, having decided to have a shower and wait quietly for my date, when I saw her. The way she was dressed, I didn't recognize her immediately. But it was her, there was no doubt about it. Her enormous breasts forced her to walk with her back arched like a show mare. She glowed with that beginning-of-the-month prosperity lap dancers have. Under her tons of jewellery, makeup, and gold-embroidered clothes pranced Debby the dancer. That was unfortunate. Usually dancers have the good taste not to work in the towns where they live. Debby had only the taste of her synthetic lavender body mist.

Faced with terror, it's fright, fight, and flight. In that order, ideally. Otherwise it can get complicated. Torn, I could see an opportunity for vengeance, but also a nice bundle of trouble wrapped up with it. She was responsible for the last thrashing I'd been served, and I hadn't even ordered it. If she hadn't interfered with my slot-machine calculations, I would have paid her for her dances. There wouldn't have been any problem. On the other hand, she would still think I was in default of payment, and might call the gorilla to her rescue. For now, there were more important questions. She was accompanied by a little boy of six at the most. Her son, probably. Sex workers reproduce, who knew? I decided to follow her and improvise as I went along. She was the owner of a lovely large muscly ass. Tailing her was a treat for the retina.

A quarter of the way around the lake, she headed toward the parking lot. I hadn't wasted anything, not even time; my car was there too. She stopped by a nearly new white SUV. The flesh trade pays well. As she was helping her son get in, I abandoned the idea of getting revenge, no longer seeing any possibility of it. I could follow her, but I'd had my fill of stalking. I was stuck behind a garbage container when providence manifested itself in the form of a small-size bladder. Debby scooped up the brat in her arms and headed toward the washrooms. Here was my chance. You have to know how to seize the opportunities you create.

I'd never punctured a tire before. It was stronger than it looked. Like me. I wanted to stick my knife in each one, but I struggled to pull the blade out of the first tire. I don't know my own strength. I'd stuck the blade in too deep. A new layer of sweat covered me. I wiggled the knife in every direction to get it out. When I finally managed it, I guessed that the brat would have finished peeing so I quickly walked back to my car. With a good angle on the SUV I wouldn't miss a single second of the scene. I was in the front row, all I needed was popcorn. The best part of revenge is savouring it.

She dragged her offspring to the truck, got him in, sat down in the driver's seat. She left the parking lot, which took me by surprise. As if nothing was wrong. I set off at speed, hampered by my injured ankle and my damp torso, which was sticking to the belt. I followed her, convinced that the tire would deflate on the road, that she'd be even more pissed. After five minutes she parked in front of a big apartment building, a poor people's co-op, and went in without further ceremony. Shit! Was my knife too thin, or her tire revenge-proof? I needed to know.

Still soaked, I pulled on my shirt and crossed the street. I leaned over the front passenger-side tire. There was no doubt—it was almost completely flat. Debby was just too stupid to notice that she was driving with a flat tire.

What are you doing there, you son of a bitch?

My heart somersaulted three times and landed on its back. In the time it took to recover from my heart attack, I'd worked out where the shout had came from. Debby was perched on a balcony on the second floor, her breasts hanging over the railing.

I know who you are, you bastard! You're the guy from the bar!

Rather than congratulate her on her powers of observation, I rushed back to my car, calling myself all the names. Everything had been just fine, all I had to do was let her leave with her flat tire and I'd have been avenged. Curiosity sabotages the noblest projects. It's well documented.

What were you doing to my truck? Hey! Stay there!

I finally managed to unlock my door and dived into my car.

I'm gonna track you down, asshole! Debby brandished a threatening fist to emphasize her words, her son hanging on her hip.

It was time to scat: a dancer in a rage is more dangerous than a bunch of peanuts in a daycare. I reversed away so that at least she couldn't get my licence plate. Especially since the car was still registered in Reynald's name; it would be a shame to get him in hot water over a hooker. I congratulated myself on the alliteration and headed back toward my place. I really needed to shower and relax before meeting Laura.

All the same, I'd have to be on my guard from then on. Even small towns are villages. Only the trees don't run into each other.

It had been a hard day under the Sherbrooke sun. Arriving back at the house I heard not only the landlord's footsteps upstairs, but also movement in the basement. Pressed against the door, I tried to figure out the situation. Had they already found me? Was it the gorilla, the police, or a new amateur baseball team wanting to practise on my head? I was intending to vigorously defend my skin and what was left of my intact bones. I walked along the little corridor, weapon in hand.

Hellooo! Aaaargh! He was more surprised than I was, which gave me the advantage. Puny and alone, he hadn't come to beat me up.

I am Apunam. I take room here. The holiday was over for me, the landlord had rented out the second room. To an Indian. Not to a real Indian from Quebec, no, an Indian from India! He probably had nothing of value to interest me. A poor immigrant around thirty with a moustache and a worn-out look. People age quickly in the sun.

Laura was lacking in the breast department. She didn't have buttocks or lips either. But she certainly had class. She'd been to university, which basically just meant she had money. She'd travelled a lot, which I would do soon. Nothing to boast about. She only drank Pu'er tea. She explained to me that, just like with wine, certain years and regions gave the best flavours. She seemed interesting, even cultivated. She didn't really excite me in genital terms but she knew how to hold a conversation on various subjects. Laura would be a good girl to introduce to my mother one day. I decided to throw myself into the seduction.

Have you ever been to India, Laura?

No, but I'd really like to go. Have you had the chance to go there?

Yes, several times, I've got a friend I stay with there when I go backpacking. His name is Apunam. He works in textiles. I immediately sensed that I was impressing her, she was playing with her hair. All the magazines say that once a girl starts playing with her hair, you're halfway there.

That's cool. Did you meet Apunam travelling? The hook was planted deep in her interest, all I had to do was reel her out of the water.

Yes, actually, during one of my trips, I went to harvest some wild Pu'er tea, the kind you like, in India. Apunam was a kind of forest guide. I trailed off, letting the silence cover me with an aura of mystery.

I don't think it's possible…

Yes, yes, it's possible. There are lots of forest guides in India. I hate it when people I'm talking to doubt me. It's rude.

No, but the tea is called Pu'er because it comes from a very particular part of China. It's a kind of regional trademark, right? That's the region it's produced in, and using a Chinese technique too. I don't think there is any in India.

Think what you like, I've been to India and picked Pu'er tea. I didn't make it up! You can ask Apunam. He's visiting Quebec. My tone didn't allow a reply. I needed to keep control of the conversation.

She replied anyway, laughing as well. *Okay, okay, I'm going to believe you even if it's unlikely. You're a special guy who does really special things, I guess. Anyway, I don't know your Indian, and I'm not going to stop every one I meet to check, ha ha!* And she took a sip of tea. I sniggered too for good measure and downed the rest of my coffee. I'd wasted enough time on her. You have to educate those arrogant university girls with your rod.

Shall we go to your place?

What?

Shall we go to your place? I've just painted the walls at my house and the smell is pretty strong. I need to air it out, it wouldn't be pleasant.

Oh, okay, I think there's been a misunderstanding. I just wanted to have tea with you, get to know you. I didn't think you had any expectations. She was playing hard to get, the tease.

I haven't got any expectations, but we're getting on well. We laughed and listened to each other plenty, didn't we? We're more intimate. We could continue the evening at your place, without expectations.

She squirmed in her chair, uncomfortable. *Yes, we've said a lot of things, but not everything, you see. I've actually got to go home to see my girlfriend.*

No problem, I'll get on well with your friend too. I was annoyed. The number of smiles and good manners I'd forced out of my body!

No, no, you don't understand. She's my girlfriend *girlfriend. My lover.* That explained why she wasn't turned on. She was dedicated to homosexuality. I smiled at her, full of complicity.

I don't have any problem with gay people, when it's two girls. Often you're not just gay, right? She stopped squirming and stiffened. I'd hit a sensitive spot, she was starting to imagine the same scene as I was. I could feel it.

Listen, I've really got to go home. Now. See you at work, okay? Stay here, finish your coffee, I'll get it. I watched her flat buttocks not swaying while she settled the bill. I'd let her stew a bit longer. I'd rattled her decision to be homosexual, that was clear. I'd work on her again in a few days.

Spending the rest of the evening alone wasn't a problem. I needed to get some cash. I even had time to detour past Mama's window beforehand. As Lil Wayne's tattoo reminds us, *Family First.*

I was eager to see my mother again, to carry on with our reunion. But in family relationships, like in sex or tea preparation, the pleasure often lies in the waiting. Rather than throwing myself into her arms, I decided to let a couple of days go by. My mother is a woman like other women, after all, she likes desire and suspense. I chose to spy on her a bit while I waited.

I'm not much of a believer, but I am religious. Walking between my usual parking spot and my observation post, I asked God to rid us of the Greek. He was poisoning my mother's life and my own at the same time. I made the most of my prayerful impulse to thank him for having led me to her. It's important to thank God. He's touchy just like everyone else. If all you do is ask him for things without thanking him, he'll end up in a sulk. Africans are a perfect example. They are a very demanding people.

I guessed that when I arrived Mama would already be sitting in front of the television, a snack close at hand. When I reached my destination, I felt my heart turn three more backflips before collapsing. It must have been the international day of coronary gymnastics. A strong light blinded me. Somebody had installed a movement detector just underneath the window. I bolted as best as I could, looking over my shoulder at the last second. The Greek was at the window, that Barabbas.

Short of breath, pain in my ribs, I set off at full throttle and smoked four cigarettes to calm down. Then a joint when I got to my bedroom. I passed Apunam coming out of the bathroom, his head down, sliding along the walls. I really wanted to hit him, bashing his face with my elbow, but I restrained myself. I needed to save my precious hatred for the Greek. And Debby's gorilla, and Mr. Paul, and the police, and all the other beneficiaries.

The landlord of the triplex must have installed the motion detector. It certainly wasn't my mother, on her waitress's wage. Or it was the Greek, worried that I'd try to get to my mother through her window. If it was him, he deserved the worst of punishments. I actually spent part of the night planning it out, involving needles, animals, hot oil, and a metal saw. Resentment prevented me from sleeping.

Reynald was still breaking my balls about the car payments. He had to make repairs on his own vehicle, his political involvement being costly in gas and I don't know what other excuse. Poor Reynald. At least save your saliva.

I know I'm going on about it, but it's really important. I was happy to help you out, but you absolutely have to give me that two hundred dollars on payday this week, okay?

Okay. We'd get paid in two days. That was my deadline. I wouldn't return to work that day, nor the days after that either. I like new experiences, but I reckoned I'd had enough work experience now. Work is crap, it's for proletarians and morons. I was worth more than that. I had my social assistance direct deposits and I managed to make it through to the end of each month with my home shopping.

No problem, Reynald. We'll go straight to Money Mart on Thursday. I knew the SPCA would have to mail my last pay-cheque to my address, at my mother's, if I didn't show up at the office again. They had legal obligations, after all. I'd just have to warn my mother. And sort things out about the Greek.

You're off again, astronaut. You travel a lot!

Yes, I went to India once.

Oh...? Right, good for you. I was just going to say that there's no time for being on another planet this morning, we've got a big day ahead of us. Reynald was putting on his having-a-bad-day airs. His candidate must have been trailing in the polls. Or he'd guessed he'd never see his money nor his car again. Or he'd realized his life was devoid of meaning. That happens from time to time.

We're going to start by rescuing a bitch and her litter from a dirty farmhouse in Compton, and then we're heading to Mégantic for a reptile shipment, a non-compliant pet shop. That'll take up our morning, and after that we'll go…

I wasn't listening anymore. We were going to Compton! A whole bunch of my favourite rappers came *straight outta Compton*! I didn't think it could be the same Compton, but I took it as a sign, it was time I moved on to serious crimes…

…and we'll finish up in Sherbrooke, cleaning the truck out, it's getting dirty.

He was right, the day was never-ending. A ton of driving under a depressing drizzle. Non-stop politics coming out of Reynald's gob. Sex, money, and my mother filling my head. Compton turned out to be pretty disappointing, of course. No ghetto, not a trace of rappers, just two or three little stores and some fields. It was after we'd got back, while we were cleaning out the truck, that the obvious hit me in the face. I'd pull off my first big stunt in Compton!

Reynald asked me what I was humming.

It's "Wicked" by Ice Cube, you won't know it.

Wicked or no wicked, scrub that corner, there's still piss there!

17

BRAVERY

On the way back I picked up a large poutine with sausage and then stopped in at the library. It was unacceptable, both the poutine and Marie-Josée's email. I must have read it twelve times before rereading it once more.

That liar had done a pretty good job of trying to convince me she was pregnant. By me, obviously. Marie-Josée assured me that she hadn't fucked anyone else for weeks, that it could only have been me, that I had to step up to my responsibilities and come back to her, that we could talk about it. She had me by the balls of my feelings.

You told me that you mist you're father so much. And you wanted to fined you're mother at all costs. Don't make you're child live that to. Marie-Josée didn't suffer from dysphasia, she was completely out of touch with language. This concerned me for the child's education, if indeed there was a child.

She'd pointlessly attached a photo of a pregnancy test; any pregnant woman might have pissed on a bit of plastic in return for a beer. It's been known to happen.

I might like to be a father one day, but I'd never start a family with a barmaid who got smashed on cocaine. And I still had things to sort out in Sherbrooke. Anyway, it was probably just a trap to get me to come back and cough up her aunt's money. Or to get revenge for her little pussy infection. What a shit email. My head was spinning.

I browsed a bit on dating sites but my heart wasn't in it. And the girls were ugly. I took down the number of the only convenience store in Compton and set off immediately. Cash would console me.

Twenty minutes before closing, I stationed myself at the elementary school, a few steps away from the store. I finished my can of beer and smoked my last cigarette. It was pretty annoying. I didn't have any cigarettes left but I couldn't exactly go and buy some at the business I was about to hold up. Too risky.

I stayed in the car. I needed to lie low until the last minute, like a jaguar. Stealing and hunting are similar arts. It's all about patience, restraint, and violence. I needed to stay focused, but the phone call with my mother was bothering me.

After I'd checked the store's closing time, I'd taken advantage of the fact that I was in an anonymous phone booth to call Mama. She had answered with a soft voice, almost smooth. *Good evening... Hello... Helloooo? I can hear breathing, is that you again? If it's you, listen to me, I don't want you to come near me again or contact me in any way, is that clear?*

She'd slammed the receiver down. It overwhelmed me, instantly carrying me back to my childhood. Her voice broken with anger and fear recalled her crises, her calls for help when she woke me up in the night. I was filled with worry. Who was she afraid of? Who was harassing her?

Was the *you* me? No, of course not, we'd only met once, and the meeting had turned out well, all things considered. It must be the Greek, that hairy Greek bastard. She'd left him at last and he couldn't accept living without her. Or she had an anonymous stalker. Beautiful women like my mother attract predators. It's well-documented. In any case, I needed to get back in touch with her, in person and soon. If she needed protecting, I was there.

Shit! I'd got lost in family concerns and time had flown. The dep was going to close any minute and I wasn't in position. I scurried round to the back of the store, avoiding the harsh light of the street lamps. I stopped behind the car parked at the side. I was ready to pop out and seize the day's takings. All my nerves were strained; so was I. I was hoping to deal with a professional and docile cashier.

I'd got there just in time. My spirits lifted when I heard the keys in the lock. Then the noise of heels coming toward the car. I leapt up and brandished my knife, shouting, *Don't move!* She wasn't at all professional, that cashier. She yelled, dropped her purse as she was putting her keys away, and ran off into the road. No word of warning, nothing, she was fleeing. All was not lost, I picked up the bag and ran as best as I could after her. I didn't want to chase her, but she was escaping in the direction of my car.

She lost a heel, fell heavily, and, seeing me approach, began screaming: *Rape! Rape!* She was crazy, no doubt about it. I was hardly going to rape her in the middle of the street.

Without stopping, I passed by her. Bag in one hand, I looked for my own keys with the other. I found them at last, dropped them, had to take off my mask to see where they had fallen, picked them up, finally managed to start driving. In the rear-view mirror I saw a man crossing the road to get to the cashier and help her up. All's well that ends well. I drove full tilt toward Sherbrooke.

I was trembling all over. The adventure had only lasted a minute but I felt as if I'd run a decathlon on my knees. My arms hurt, and my thighs, and my ankle, and I was crying. And I still don't even know why. Maybe it was joy at having pulled off my first holdup. Even though that was a legitimate reason, it was embarrassing.

On the outskirts of Sherbrooke I passed two police cars, lights flashing. As I suspected, Compton was just far enough away that I could benefit from the delay. I thought one of the cars did a U-turn when I passed, but I charged ahead without stopping at any traffic lights. Nobody caught up with me. In no time I was back at the house, stretched out on my bed, trying to catch my breath and clutching the bag against my chest.

This time, the surprise bag was worth the trouble. Straight-away I found a pack of cigarettes. They were menthols, but that was better than nothing. I lit one. There were also several condoms, which turned me on. Tons of useless papers, makeup I could give to my mother, and finally, money, lots of money. Only a few dollars in the wallet, but, as expected, an envelope intended for the bank with the day's takings. Three hundred and forty beautiful dollars. I threw them into the air like they do in films. Then I had the nuisance of collecting them from the four corners of the room on all fours. I thought I was celebrating the first holdup in a long series. It was more stressful than going shopping in empty houses, but nothing ventured, not much gained.

The night had been profitable, but the day weighed heavily on me. I had problems up to here—the whole thing with my mother being harassed and the hypothetical baby Marie-Josée wanted to pin on me. But above all, I had pockets full of money. I had even fewer reasons to go and bore myself to death in the truck with Reynald, even if the truck was nice and clean. All I could think of was finding a bar, downing a few pills, some pints of beer, and playing on the machines. I felt sure luck would be smiling on me.

Reynald wasn't in a good mood either. It was another grey day with annoying drizzle. Either be rainy or let the sun shine.

Nothing is worse than grey areas and half measures. You can't even figure out how fast to set the windshield wipers in that weather.

You must have had a rough night, young man. Reynald started up a conversation like a true Watson.

No, quite the opposite, but I feel like I'm going to have a bad day. I emphasized my words by swishing saliva between my teeth. It makes a very particular little sound. Haitians often do it. I love it.

Is the temperature bothering you? Personal problems? And off we went for another round with Reynald the amateur psychologist. I decided to play his game to kill some time.

I got some bad news about my mother. She's having problems with her ex, he's harassing her. I emphasized *harassing* so he would understand the seriousness of the situation.

Breakups are never easy. You should remind your mother to set limits. At least that way it'll be clear from her side. He could even play the psychologist through an intermediary, good for him.

Yes, I'll tell her that. Where are we going now? I cut the session short. I intended to set my own limits for my mother's ex, and Reynald was getting on my nerves. He too was getting close to seeing my limits. I'd played the nice guy long enough with him.

We're going to City Hall, a family of skunks has moved into the archives room. We need to take things carefully. We'll put them to sleep with pills mixed with ground meat. If that doesn't work, we'll have to use darts. He turned toward me so I'd feel the weight of the next sentence. *This time* I'll *use the darts.*

Working is hard enough, but hanging about waiting is far more difficult. We were right downtown, I saw three bars from the truck where we were sitting around. Reynald thought we'd have to give it half an hour before checking to see if the creatures had eaten their meat, which we'd seasoned with sleeping pills. He hoped he'd put enough in to put the mother to sleep. The little ones' glands were probably not developed yet, but if the mother let rip in the city archives, nobody would be consulting them for a good few years. It was a major contract, City Hall, we couldn't afford to make a mistake.

Do you want to go back to that breakfast place for lunch? I feel like an omelette. He was rubbing his paunch. Reynald seemed vulgar to me, I didn't want my mother to see me with him again.

No, I'd rather buy sandwiches from the supermarket. We could just take half an hour and then finish earlier. On that note, I got out of the truck to smoke a menthol. It tasted like ass, menthol ass. Nothing could please me that morning, I didn't like work anymore, or Reynald, or myself. I was obsessed with gambling, alcohol, and my mother. I hoped nothing bad was going to happen to her.

Reynald stayed in the truck, listening to the news, nodding his head or shaking it according to the story. I smoked three more cigarettes before he hauled himself out of the vehicle and decided to check out the results of his meatballs.

There was nothing left. Reynald had put two meatballs in each of the three long rows in the archives, in the basement. Not a single pellet in the first row. Not a single pellet in the second row and not a single pellet in the third row, just a big dead skunk with her four little ones skittering around her, one of which was trying to nurse.

Oh! We won't be needing the darts, after all. I think your meat must have gone bad.

He shot me a look of wounded innocence. Choked up, he leaned over the skunk, feeling it, trying to find a scrap of life where there was nothing left except the result of his mistake, death. *Go and look for the cage instead of looking for trouble!*

I didn't have to take orders from Reynald, and especially not in that tone. I stayed right in front of him and held his gaze.

What's up with you this morning, you damn moron? Go and get the cage so we can take the little ones.

I was very mature. Instead of smashing his skull open with my heels, I invited him to stuff the cage in question deep inside himself and I left. Somebody even opened the door for me. A lady in a suit, visibly bothered by our altercation, was coming to make sure everything was alright.

Not for your skunk, ma'am! I slammed the door behind me, leaving her with a defeated Reynald.

I was drinking Goldschläger. It makes your breath smell good. When I drink before noon I avoid strong-smelling alcohol. Especially since I was planning on visiting my mother around three o'clock. I guessed she must finish her shift around that time. Some men drink to give themselves courage, which is nonsense. You either have courage or you don't. And I do have it. Drinking strong liquor just helps me control my stress levels.

I was anxious about seeing my mother again, of course, but even more so because of my worries about the Greek. Did I need to take his threats seriously? You never know. Those who bark rarely bite, but when they do bite they take your whole leg off. I didn't know a thing about the guy, maybe he had the means to match his ambitions. I was also stressed about my algorithm, which wasn't paying out. I'd already given the machine a dozen times twenty bucks. With the shots and the tips I was giving the beautiful Sonya, my savings were melting away.

I needed to focus, I had to only increase the bet when three bells or more appeared on the screen. In principle, that should pay out two times out of four. I played and I lost. I put another twenty in. Thanks to the amphetamine I'd taken in the washrooms, time was racing past at top speed. I put in another twenty. And another one. I put in my last twenty and there was nothing left in my pockets.

But all of a sudden I won four hundred and twenty dollars! Bells in the four corners, bells in a diamond shape, bells all round the screen, all the fucking bells I could ever need! I swallowed my saliva with difficulty, as well as my desire to shout for joy. I noted with pleasure the jealousy on the face of the poor old woman who was on the machine right next to mine. *Four hundred and twenty dollars, old gal, that would get you back on track!* I kept this thought to myself, but I was exulting inside. *An orgasm is never as good when you hold back,* wrote Romain Gary. Well, I held back and had a great orgasm, Romain! My algorithm worked, the proof was right there. I could clean out all the slot machines and casinos in the province. Anything was possible.

Sonya and I celebrated with big glasses of Goldschläger. She invited me to join her in some cocaine, which seems to be a real obsession among barmaids, but I refused. I'm a responsible man. I had to go and meet my mother. That was my top priority, as the big shots say. But I promised to come back that evening and sniff a few flakes off her generous chest, as well as my broken nose could manage, anyway. After a bit of tongue tennis I left the bar, one foot in front of the other with a little sideways jerk.

The midday sun is harsh on people of the shade. I needed to get that thought written down; it would make a good title for a poetry collection. Publishing poetry must pay well, it's a noble endeavour. A good Quebec poet must be looking at six figures. There must also be a great brotherhood of poets, and tons of women wanting to pose naked to inspire them. Yes, I was going to write some poetry, between a couple of rap albums. And with the income from the machines as well I'd be sure to make an absolute killing and go down in history. If you're going to be in the world, might as well make your mark on it.

For now, though, the sun was putting me into a daze and I noticed that the alcohol had got me pretty intoxicated. I was having a bit of trouble walking. Luckily my car was parked close by. I ought to go home for a nap before meeting Mama.

I piss sitting down. First off, it's cleaner, and it's also the thinker's position. The bathroom is a place of contemplation. In the pleasure of relieving a bladder ready to burst, there's also the pleasure of meditation. When I got home, I hurtled down the stairs to the bathroom in the desire to liberate my body of a double tension. And I sat in piss. Yes, someone had pissed on the toilet. My desire vanished in an instant, leaving only the desire to drag Apunam by the moustache and shove his face in it. For educational purposes.

I burst into his bedroom with a single kick to the door. He sat bolt upright in bed, pointing a long blade at me. He stammered some Indian creole interspersed with *Non no non no non.* I have to admit, the knife cooled my ardour. It was a decent blade, a good ten or twelve inches of steel, double-edged and everything. Practically a sword. I wondered if he'd acquired the weapon after our first meeting when I pulled one on him, to get back at me, or if he was just naturally defensive.

Keep calm and do your shit, one of my favourite shirts says. Made in India too. I didn't let myself get confused and I yelled at Apunam, telling him he had to piss sitting down from now on. He understood nothing, his French immersion was not complete. To help him, I mimed a man holding his penis to urinate then drying off the organ with vigorous movements. He seemed even more frightened than he had when I arrived and repeated *Non no no non* as he crouched in his bed. He thought I wanted to fuck him, the idiot.

Listen to me, Apunam. Tu m'understand?

No no non! Don't, don't!

Keep calm! I don't want you to piss on the toilet. Is it clear? Je suis clair?

No no!

Yes! Listen me, je te dis! Yes you piss don't on the toilet, okay? Yes?

Yes, yes, mister. He was on the verge of tears, poor Apunam. He was shaking all over. No need to get so worked up about a drop of peepee on the toilet. All roommates have little misunderstandings from time to time. Apunam was sensitive.

I left him to think about it, politely closing the door behind me. I went back to attend to my little needs, promising myself that I'd steal his dagger off him at the first opportunity.

Relieved, I went back to my room and calmed myself down in no time.

I had a nightmare I could remember nothing about. It's worse when you can't remember. I got up with a heavy empty feeling in my chest and a general sense of fear. A little worse for wear from the morning's series of strong drinks too. I quickly got my emotions under control by feeling my pants pockets. I had a nice wad but, more importantly, proof that my theory was right. I was keen to play again to get even richer, get back everything the machines had stolen from me in the past and then make my profit margin explode.

Drunk on enthusiasm, I was amazed when I saw the time. It was almost 6:00 p.m. That was more than just a nap I'd had. I must have accumulated some tiredness. Thinking back, I realized that the last three weeks had been very busy and that I hadn't really slept much. But I also thought it was emotions that had tired me out. Emotions are physical. Like we did in the group workshops in the secure centre, I tried to identify all the emotions I'd been through in the last twenty-four hours. With the holdup, work, gambling win, and the prospective visit to my mother, it was all too much, I was losing the plot.

I carried on thinking about it in the shower. Moods are really not reliable. It takes nothing to plunge you into the depths or make you soar. But by the grace of God we have drugs, medicines, and alcohol to stabilize us. I smoked my last menthol fag in front of the mirror and doused myself in cologne. I still had a few red marks on my face, and purple and yellow marbling on my ribs, but I was getting much better. With the tattoo on my neck, I looked like a real mafioso, rich and sexy. I pulled on my nicest shirt, the one with flames on it, and left the house.

I was about to get into my car when the landlady called me. She was standing by the main entrance, with her hair pulled back, and wearing sweatpants. She signalled to me to join her. No class, that old lady. She must have inherited the house. I'd bet she'd never worked.

I told you, I'm going to give you two weeks' rent on Saturday. I used my half-conciliatory, half-exasperated voice, the tenant's usual tone.

Yes, you sure do have to pay me on Saturday, but I want to know what happened with the new guy.

The Indian guy? I was surprised.

Yes, the Indian guy. Unless someone's renting a room from me in secret, there's just the two of you. He wants to leave and wants me to return his rent for the week. He was almost crying, what happened between you two? She was frowning. That's to add emphasis.

No idea, I don't know what you're talking about. Maybe he's got little girl lungs, it's damp down there. I stepped away from her immediately and gave her a little nod, polite but firm. I had to leave.

We'll talk about this another time. Don't forget to pay me on Saturday, we're not supposed to give credit.

I thanked her and sped off right away. So he was Indian with a bit of squealer mixed in, little Apunam. He would pay for this.

On the way I stopped at the dep. I'm always so reluctant to buy cigarettes. It's robbery, especially when you pay the maximum taxes. They don't keep them behind the counter for nothing, they know people would steal them just to keep the state from getting rich. I often steal alcohol or sweets to compensate.

I was slipping two bars of chocolate into my pocket when I heard my name, my real name. Frozen, I turned round and came face to face with Jenny, the fat girl, who'd slimmed down since my stay with her foster family. A lot. She was almost pretty. I played the interested card, and said I was amazed to see her in town, wanted to know all the details, and so on and so on. She was studying in Sherbrooke, political science. Her parents were well, she'd say hi to them. Rocket had been dead for three years.

I'm really sorry, Jenny.

Yeah, he was important to us. He was a member of the family.

I was going to point out that he was the only one who wasn't obese, but I decided to hold back, it might wreck my chances of luring her. I searched for a catchy subject to fuel the conversation, while stroking her breasts in my head the whole time. *All my condolences. He was a good dog.* It's useful to go on about your target's life so that she feels interesting and unique.

Yes, thanks… I don't know if you know, but not long after you left, Benjamin committed suicide. She turned away slightly at the end of the sentence, as if she regretted having said it.

Did he completely commit suicide?

What do you mean, completely?

Um… All the way, did he die? In my family's experience, suicide was a long journey, a process requiring transportation by ambulance, hospitalizations, and treatment. You didn't kill yourself just like that.

Yes, he died, at the house. We stopped being a foster family after that.

I was listening to her, really, when they signalled that it was my turn. I asked the cashier for two packs, all the while searching for something to reel Jenny in. I couldn't do it, Benjamin's face kept coming into my head. Before and after Steve and I beat him up. It's stupid to commit suicide, especially when you're young.

You shouldn't die before you've started to live.

I slipped the cigarettes into my pocket and asked Jenny if she wanted to go out for a drink to catch up. Maybe more, if I could conjure up some things we had in common. My grief over Benjamin was all done and I was coming back to the important things—my needs. Jenny turned down the invitation, claiming she had too much studying. I wanted to get her number or set up a date, but she replied that she'd rather just leave things there, that it would be too weird to see each other again. She'd lost fifty pounds for nothing, she was still a total loser.

18

PERSEVERANCE

When I arrived at my mother's, I wasn't doing well. This meeting seemed crucial. We'd broken the ice, and now we had to dive together into the cold waters of reunion. Mama must have shared my fears. She'd have to invite me into her house, it was a big deal. She'd tell me not to look at the mess and feel bad that she didn't have anything good to offer me even though her fridge was overflowing with delicious food. Maybe she'd want to keep me for the night. I'd refuse. Not the first night.

I stayed on the sidewalk, images of the upcoming meeting playing in my mind. I must have loitered for an hour, minimum. Deep in my subconscious, I really wanted her to see me and come out to me. I wanted her to cross the road, or at least give me a wave through the window. But the curtains were drawn. It was still early though.

I was afraid of the Greek being there too, even if I didn't dare admit it to myself. I'm not a pussy and it was useless to think about it. In life, you have to get going without asking yourself too many questions. Questions give birth to doubts and doubts attract trouble. Once you've made up your mind, you need to run at the wall until it falls over. I'm a decisive man. I was going to meet my mother that evening. I smoked a last joint while chewing gum, for my breath.

Of course it was Zorba who answered the door. He accompanied his welcome with a typical Quebec curse. The Greek was assimilating. I spotted my mother behind him, on the phone. *It's him, it's him,* she was repeating. She must have been talking to one of my aunts or someone else in the family, impatient to see me.

Hairy Guy was just a splinter in my way. I moved forward and pushed him with one hand. He didn't move. The splinter was turning out to be a real pain in the arse, as the English say. He surprised me and pushed me off the little porch. I hurtled backwards down the steps but didn't fall. I made sure he knew that.

Bravo, big guy, I didn't even fall over! I noticed my voice was a bit hoarse. It was a bit lacking in presence.

Shut your mouth, for Christ's sake! Greeks are very religious, it's a genetic thing.

He jumped the three steps to join me right at the entrance to the yard. I was leaning on, or maybe even pushed up against, my mother's car and checking out my options. I hadn't come to fight, I'd had more than enough of that over the past few weeks. My mother wanted to see me, I could feel it. I wanted to see her too, it was basically all I wanted. Maybe she was being kept prisoner. In any case, her big controlling Greek was an obstacle. I had to find a way around him.

If I could get into the apartment and close the door behind me, I'd have a moment of peace with my mother—we could shut ourselves away together. At the very least, we'd have time to arrange a secret meeting somewhere else. I needed to sneak into the apartment before the Greek could catch me. With a great leap, I took a run up and was immediately knocked down. The barbarian had smashed me in the temple.

I'd only put one knee down on the ground, it wasn't exactly a KO. I got up and raised my guard. *You big jerk, let me see my mother!*

But she isn't your mother! Understand? Go and get help!

Words hurt more than blows. He needed to shut up at all costs, even if I didn't believe anything coming out of his piehole. I didn't want his words to stain me, to sully our reunion, he needed to shut up. I tried to grab his face but he punched me before I could reach him. *Not the nose, fucking fuck, not the nose!* The nose.

I could taste my blood, it was flowing over my lips and down my throat. But I hadn't fallen. My honour was safe. Through the veil of tears, I saw him turn toward my mother. One of his hairy arms took her by the shoulder and pulled her back inside. Her arms. All I wanted was an embrace from my mother.

The braggart's last words rolled around inside my head. *We called the police. They're looking for you.* I needed to leave quickly. I wiped my lips with my right hand and left a trail of blood on Mama's white car. I was leaving a bit of myself for her. Blood and regret. Even in the midst of tragedy I'm a great romantic.

I made it to the end of the block stopping up my nose. It was futile, it was pouring out between my fingers in surges and leaving a track behind me. I was just getting to my car when I heard sirens wailing. He really had called the pigs, the bastard. I wondered if my mother had tried to stop him. I also wondered about this tale of their looking for me. Why were they looking for me? How had he known?

My revenge would be dreadful. My hatred was taking on gargantuan proportions. Between the Greek and me, things were personal now.

The next morning, the mirror did not find me fair at all. I no longer looked like a mafioso but a one-armed boxer at the end of a long career. I'd hoped the night might make things better, especially my nose. On the contrary, it was more crooked than my teeth and my mind, which is saying something. The standard collateral damage, black eyes, had come back. Or purple eyes, in my case.

As I left the bathroom I met Apunam, on his way to shut himself in his bedroom with a bowl of cereal. The handle wasn't fixed yet so I went in. He choked on his cereal. If that's any indication of the strength of the emerging power, we're fine. A real chickenshit. I asked him, with the aid of signs, if he had a phone. He could hardly get it out of his pocket, he was shaking so much. He must have thought wounds were contagious, poor guy. I thanked him and called my mother. The tragedy had gone on long enough. I wanted to meet up with her that morning, far away from her jailer.

The Greek had such a hold over my mother that her phone line was out of service. He must have had the number changed. Yet more confirmation of the conjugal violence my mother was trapped in. I'd seen a report on it. Violent men like him isolate their victims. They cut their bridges with their networks, their friends, and of course their family.

I had to get my mother out of that wasps' nest.

I arrived at the restaurant, determined to leave on my mother's arm. She could live in my room or we'd rent one at the hotel if she couldn't stand Apunam. From that morning on, she'd be free of domestic violence.

Her car wasn't in the parking lot. That was a bad sign. I realized that people were plotting against me, that her colleagues were in league with her executioner. All the waitresses were staring at me, and not just because I was wounded so fantastically. I could see the suspicion and the fear in their cruel little eyes. I noticed one on the phone, hidden away behind a pillar. She was probably an informer. She must have been in communication with the Greek or the police. I left so I'd be able to come back again. My revenge list was turning into a phone directory.

Mama wasn't at her house either. Where could he have shut her away? I didn't know his name or his address. I couldn't look up everyone in the phone book with a Greek last name. Anyway, he might be from a different hairy tribe and not even Greek. I'd have to ask Apunam about that.

You're never as alone as when you're by yourself. I had nobody to confide in, nobody to contact, and my mother was in danger. I wanted to talk. Worse still, I needed to. I was drowning in a rancid slop of emotions. Even the psychologists who ran the emotional management workshops couldn't have identified them all, there were so many of them. I was hurt, worried, afraid, and loads of other feelings too, no doubt.

All my plans had been turned upside down. I wasn't supposed to go back to work, especially since it was payday. I now realized the impossibility of getting my paycheque sent to Prospect Street. It would be intercepted. I needed to go to work and get it in my own hands. I could make things up with Reynald and, at the same time, confide in him, in guarded words. I even imagined doing one last day of work. Despite our clashes, I'd got pretty attached to old Reynald. I'd just have to come up with some way of not paying him what I owed him.

When I arrived at work I was already feeling better. I was expecting a warm welcome from the other employees. When they saw my face, they'd never get over how I'd defended a girl from being attacked in the park by two masked men. Laura would be especially impressed.

The welcome was cold. A little closed circle was already having a confab, and they barely turned toward me. Just enough to show me their surprised and suspicious looks. That was the day's theme. I passed close by Laura, proudly, and I took the truck keys from the counter.

What are you doing? She wasn't that beautiful, it turned out. Especially with her pinched responsible-adult look.

I'm taking the keys to the truck. Reynald is late. I'll wait for him outside. I tried to come up with a subtle insult, a wounding remark to finish up with. I didn't have to answer to this lesbian.

No, Reynald was on time. But two police officers were waiting for him. One of his cars was seen at the location of a robbery. If it's the one he sold you, you're probably better off waiting here or calling the station.

Shit! *It's possible, the car was stolen.*

What? Really? She leaned over to get a better look out at the parking lot.

Before she could see the car, I took back control of the situation, under the hostile stares of the other two girls.

My Indian roomate stole it. I managed to find him and get it back, but I have no idea what he did with it.

Your Indian Chinese-tea-picker? The frown suited her even less than the pinched look. No, Laura wasn't pretty at all.

Yes, that's right. That's the one. Anyway, there's work to be done, then I have to wash the truck. If the police call I'm available, but on the road. I'll come back, if need be. I was sweating like a pig at the beach.

Wait, you've got no right! Laura followed me outside, the other snooty girls behind her. I collected my cigarettes and my last amphetamines from the car, and said my goodbyes to it. It was my first car, after all.

No, you can't leave with the truck. I need to call Carole first. The others nodded in agreement. The director's approval was needed.

Reynald told me I was ready to drive the truck and work alone. Call me if something happens. I'll come back for Reynald when he gets back. I pushed Laura away, successfully.

She was still whining, tapping on my window while I was heading for the road. And there we were, just like in the books, just like in the films. I was on the run.

The truck had several advantages. I could easily sleep comfortably in it, the gas tank was full, and, most important, I had access to anaesthetic products, including most notably the tranquilizer gun. I could make use of it to hold up a store or defend myself against the police, if they found me.

Predictably, Laura called me just a few minutes later. The radio crackled before emitting her nasal little voice. *Call from the centre. Come back immediately! There's an emergency, you have to come back to the centre. Reply. Reply, please… Reynald has got back.* Oh, fuck off. I was sure she'd already alerted the pigs.

I needed to be efficient. Adrenaline wouldn't be enough. I swallowed two amphetamines to focus my mind. The car had been seen, but where? Were they looking for me for a burglary or the holdup? Under which identity? When would I see my mother again? I was chain-smoking. It was forbidden in the truck. But nothing was forbidden anymore, I was in survival mode.

Before leaving—or fleeing, to be more precise—I decided to gather my possessions and anything else that seemed useful from the house. When I got there, I heard Apunam shut himself in his bedroom. I headed to my own room, stuffed everything I could find in my sports bag and my backpack. Next, I broke down Apunam's door with two solid kicks. He'd pushed a desk against the door but I soon managed to move it and invade his lair. He was standing in a corner of the bedroom, pale with terror. He was holding his long dagger, the object of my desire, to himself. He didn't dare point it anymore.

Give it to me, Apunam.

No, non.

GIVE IT TO ME, J'AI DIT! My hand held out toward him, I moved a couple of steps forward. He let the knife drop on the ground, stifling a little squeak. Apunam was adorable.

I picked up the weapon and waved it in his direction. *You move don't, okay? You stay. Tu restes là. Reste, Apunam!*

That was pointless. As I left the bedroom, I heard the landlady, panic-stricken, phoning for help. The police, probably. She'd have been better off calling a cabinet maker, the pigs were already on the case anyway, and she had a half-off door in the basement. I'd be long gone in five minutes.

I used the back of a cigarette package to write a note to my mother. Words are never easy to find when they're hiding behind emotions. I was looking for a shock phrase, the right formula that would make her understand all the regret I felt about leaving her for the time being. I tried to write her a poem with pretty rhymes, but I couldn't manage it. Time was limited. Too bad. I concentrated on the essentials.

I'll find you again, I will always find you again. I'll come back soon. I love you, Mama. That would reassure her.

I was going to drop off these loving words then take off, that was the plan. Once I arrived at the corner of her street, I noticed a patrol car in front of the building. The bastards were even stopping me from leaving my mother a goodbye note. I retraced my steps, promising myself I'd mail the note and a poem as soon as I could.

I had to avoid the highways, that's where they'd be waiting for me. I needed to go through the villages. For now, I had to get across town. I took the back streets through Sherbrooke, knowing them well by now. I ripped out the radio, Laura's cursing was irritating me. I listened to the news, but they weren't talking about my escape yet.

As I went along Montreal Street, I spotted three cats on a balcony. It was Mrs. Picard's balcony! The crazy lady had finished psychiatry and had started collecting again. I stepped on the brake, twisted my neck to get a better look. It really was her apartment. I saw a fourth cat in the window. Then a fifth! A surge of anger washed over me and my sense of duty was aroused. I needed to set those cats free and educate that crazy lady.

I know, I know, it was insane. I should have carried on driving, just got out of there. But it was stronger than I was. We'd warned her to stop her nonsense; she wasn't allowed to have cats anymore. She wasn't respecting our authority and was exposing animals to danger.

I'd do it fast, give her a roasting and liberate the cats. I'd keep one of them for the road. It would keep me company. That's what I wanted to do. That was all I wanted to do, spend a few minutes sorting her out and then head off again, without hurting anybody.

I thought about taking her hostage too, if the police spotted the truck. If not, freeing the cats would be my last professional act, my swan song of the job. I ran across the road and climbed the stairs four at a time, wrecking my ankle again. I knocked on her door and, to my great astonishment, she opened it right away. She recognized my shirt with the SPCA logo and tried to close it again, but I blocked the door with my foot and shoved my way in with my shoulder. My doing that knocked her over; she fell on the living room table and then to the floor. She was whimpering. *My kitties, my kitties.* A few starving ones were already taking advantage of the open door and racing off down the stairs.

I'd imagined her as being taller, sturdier too. She was a skinny, dry little woman, Mrs. Picard, practically fragile. Her fuchsia dressing gown was open over a pale body. The image disturbed me.

The smell of piss and ammonia, less intense than last time, was still striking. I summarized what I thought of her in a few short, dynamic sentences. I left her on the floor and went to open the doors to the bedroom and the bathroom. Half a dozen cats rushed out, ignoring the crazy lady's pleas. She got up and tried to catch them. I glanced quickly around the room. There was nothing valuable left, as expected.

Feeling merciful, I was going to leave without further ado. For my trouble, I'd take a cat from near the building door as I liberated the others. But that was without taking the old dame's anger into account. She threw herself at me, wailing like a woman possessed, scratching my face and arms. *My kitties, my kitties!*

I'd been on the receiving end of too many blows in too short a time. Everyone has their limits.

I should have stopped after the first head butt, but I was filled with fear, hatred, and I don't know what else. I had blood in my eyes, hers and mine. I was sweating and disoriented. My mind was really altered too, I must confess. The amphetamines had sharpened more than just my brain.

I should have left. The police would be showing up any minute. I needed to get out of there as fast as possible. I panicked. For the first time in my life, I lost control. I hit her without stopping. Her face, her ribs, her stomach, and then her face again. It was a nightmare, I was hitting with all my strength, but it was as if my blows weren't reaching their mark, as if I was beating the air. In spite of the pain in my wrists and knuckles, in spite of all the blood splattering and blinding me, I needed to hit harder and harder, more and more, with each blow. I was a rusty spring rediscovering its strength. I think everything had just been too much for me. It was all pouring out. It wasn't her fault. I didn't want to kill her personally. But I couldn't stop hitting. A thousand blows.

A stabbing pain pierced my chest, a point under the ribs on my left side. I had to pause to get my breath back. It was enough to stop me completely. Mrs. Picard was inert, but moaning loudly. I left her on the floor, closed the apartment door, which had stayed partly open the whole time. I wound up in the kitchen and got myself a glass of cold water. I remained sitting at the table for a few long seconds, moody, wondering why she'd panicked like that, why she'd thrown herself at me like a lunatic. I kept telling myself they ought to have locked her up in the psychiatric hospital and then I realized they'd be wanting to lock me up too—in prison.

She was moaning less and less, choking on her blood from time to time. She was dying, probably. I was still hesitating a bit between pleading legitimate defence and madness. The police would be there any minute. I needed to act quickly.

I got closer to her and heard her last breath. I think it was a relief for both of us. I moved a kitten away that was busily licking her face and then ran two fingers over her split lips. Even though the blood had started to coagulate, my fingers were wet. Wet enough to write on the white living room wall. I had to return for more of this organic ink three times before I was done.

Amazed that the police still hadn't arrived, and having no idea how much time had passed, I told myself that escape was still possible. And I certainly wasn't planning on making myself a cake while I waited to be arrested. I'm not responsible for police incompetence.

Before I fled, I made a little sign of the cross for Lucie. I'd learned her name when I took the little chain she was wearing round her wrist. The body was called Lucie Picard. Two cats were keeping her company and licking her wounds. I took a last look back at my graffiti, *IT WAS THE CATS' FAULT*, and then I closed the door behind me.

EPILOGUE

They say that only fools never change their minds. I changed mine. Pleading madness would be complicated and dishonest. And the biggest risk was ending up in a psychiatric institution. Turns out that's not what I want. There wouldn't be any promising contacts to make there. I'd rather meet Russians and Italians in a good old-fashioned prison. Even if it means broadening my sexual horizons. I'm ready to do hard time.

This is why I'm putting everything down in writing, so that people know where I'm coming from and understand that I'm completely aware of my actions. I also want my mother to hear this account at the trial, so she knows all the effort I went to trying to find her, to be with her. I confess, I also hope that someone might see a book or movie in my experience, but that would be a secondary benefit.

I've been writing without stopping for three days now. Marie-Josée couldn't believe it when I showed up at her place. As for me, I wasn't surprised to discover that the pregnancy test turned out to be a fabrication. I wasn't surprised, but I was still sad. I'd have liked to be a father. I know I'd have been a good father, present and gentle. Marie-Josée told me she'd lost it. I lost my cool, again.

After a lie like that I feel well within my rights to use her computer and her apartment. I untie her a bit sometimes so we can make love.

I follow the investigation's progress in the news. Not much is happening, they found the truck at the mall and broadcast my photo from the Sherbrooke public library on every channel. There must be a whole team of inspectors and a tactical division on my case. It won't be much longer.

There are only a few amphetamines left to swallow and the fridge is nearly empty. I don't have any money left to feed Marie-Josée and her cat. It would be stupid if they starved to death. On the other hand, I can't turn myself in. That would totally discredit me with the mafia. It just isn't done.

I've got nothing left to write. I'm going to wait another hour and then I'll go and hold up another store, if the police don't get here before then. I have no choice, I only have three cigarettes left.

I'm a responsible man. I'm going to face the consequences of my actions. I welcome the sentence. I'll do my time. But you know the worst thing about prison? No animals allowed.

ACKNOWLEDGEMENTS

First of all, I would like to thank all the weirdos who inspired me.
Also, Marie-Eve Gélinas, Carole Boutin
and the incredible team at Groupe Librex.
JC Sutcliffe for the great translation, tu es formidable
(en français dans le texte)!
The wonderful Hazel and Jay from Book*hug.
And you, dear open-minded reader, you rock!
PS: this is the first book of a trilogy; collect them all!

—D.G.

Thank you to Christopher Dummitt, David Goudreault,
Marie-Eve Gélinas, Hazel Millar, Jay MillAr,
Stuart Ross, Pablo Strauss.

—J.S.

ABOUT THE AUTHOR

Marianne Deschênes

DAVID GOUDREAULT is a novelist, poet and song-writer. He was the first Quebecer to win the World Cup of Slam Poetry in Paris, France. David leads creative workshops in schools and detention centres across Quebec—including the northern communities of Nunavik—and in France. He has received a number of prizes, including Quebec's Medal of the National Assembly for his artistic achievements and social involvement and the Grand Prix littéraire Archambault for his first novel, *La Bête à sa mère* (*Mama's Boy*). He is also the author of *La bête et sa cage* and *Abattre la bête*, both of which will appear in English translation from Book*hug. He lives in Sherbrooke, Quebec.

———

JC SUTCLIFFE is a writer, translator, book reviewer, and editor. She has lived in England, France, and Canada.

COLOPHON

Manufactured as the first English edition of *Mama's Boy*
in the spring of 2018 by Book*hug.

Distributed in Canada by the Literary Press Group: lpg.ca

Distributed in the United States by Small Press Distribution:
spdbooks.org

Shop online at bookthug.ca

BOOK
PRODUCTION
WAR ECONOMY
STANDARD

Type + design by Tree Abraham
Copy edited by Stuart Ross